THRILL KILLER!

Hoover swiftly slid out of the saddle and pounced on the guns before Gabe could recover from the brutal blow. There was a smile on Hoover's face when he fired off a pair of rounds.

One of them tore into Gabe's upper right thigh, bringing piercing pain and smashing Gabe to the earth.

Hoover walked toward him twirling the guns in his hands. "I'm going to shoot you to death," he announced, still grinning. "But slow and easy. First I'm going to shoot you in the other leg. Then in the arms. Then in the gut. I'm going to fill you so full of holes you can be used for a sieve when I'm through with you."

LONG RIDER

★ WANTED DEAD OR ALIVE ★

CLAY DAWSON

DIAMOND BOOKS, NEW YORK

This book is a Diamond original edition, and has never been previously published.

WANTED DEAD OR ALIVE

A Diamond Book/published by arrangement with the author

PRINTING HISTORY
Diamond edition/November 1993

ISBN: 1-55773-961-7

Diamond Books are published by The Berkley Publishing Group, 200 Madison Avenue, New York, NY 10016.
DIAMOND and the "D" design
are trademarks belonging to Charter Communications, Inc.

PRINTED IN THE UNITED STATES OF AMERICA

10 9 8 7 6 5 4 3 2 1

LONG RIDER

★ WANTED DEAD OR ALIVE ★

CHAPTER ONE

"Go git 'im!" Wes Harrison yelled at the top of his voice. "Go git 'im, Gabe!"

Gabe Conrad slammed spurs into his horse's flanks, and the dapple responded with a burst of speed that took horse and rider up a steep slope. As they topped it, the cow Gabe had been chasing raced down into the draw on the other side where once a stream had flowed.

Gabe gripped his mount with his knees as the horse skidded down the slope on its haunches. When it hit bottom and had gotten to its feet again, Gabe turned it and raced down the draw after the cow, which was clattering across the stones that filled the dry streambed.

Wes appeared on top of the slope, his horse circling. "Hey, Gabe, how's it feel to have a bellyful of bedsprings?"

Gabe grinned in response to Wes's laughter. The man was right, he thought, as he galloped after the cow that was nearing the end of the draw. This broken country had a way of bouncing both the brains and belly out of a man.

As if to prove him right, the ground beneath his horse's hooves sprouted a rough series of cuts and ruts running at all angles. Gabe's dapple stumbled and almost threw him, but he held tightly to the reins and gripped the horse even harder with his legs. The dapple regained its balance and plowed on, its iron shoes striking sparks from the stones it was traveling over. Then horse and rider were up and out of the draw and traveling across fairly level ground, which was dotted with thick stands of scrub.

Gabe slowed his mount when he realized his quarry had vanished. Now where the hell . . .

He scanned the surrounding countryside, but all he could see were other mounted men like himself riding hard in pursuit of strays. There was no sign of the cow he had, it seemed to him, been chasing over hill and dale for hours. Actually, it had been only minutes. But the hot sun and the rough country made it seem much longer.

Gabe muttered an oath. He spurred his dapple to send it galloping toward the scrub growing nearest to them. On the way to it, he reached behind him and freed his slicker from his bedroll. When they reached their destination, he turned the dapple at a sharp right angle and simultaneously flailed the scrub with his slicker.

The tactic worked. Out of the scrub lumbered the cow he had been after. It threw its tail up into the air and went running away from its pursuer. It let out a bawl as it fled. Gabe let out a roar and went after it, whirling his slicker above his head as he did so.

Soon he had shortened the distance between himself and the cow. But the cow was not ready to give up yet. As Gabe closed in on it, it veered to the left, turned, and went running back the way it had come, its head down, its tail still up.

Gabe used the reins to turn his horse, but then he dropped them to the saddle horn and relaxed the pressure he had been applying with his knees. The horse responded as Gabe had thought he would. The dapple increased its speed until it was traveling at a full gallop as it went after the cow.

"Do it," Gabe said aloud to his mount. "Don't mind me. I'm just along for the ride."

The dapple's ears twitched. Its gaze remained glued to the cow just ahead of it.

I was just getting in your way with those reins, Gabe thought, as the dapple under him streaked forward and he swayed in the saddle. I'll give you your head, and you can show me how good a cutting horse you really are.

The dapple swerved the instant the cow up ahead of it swerved. It turned again without breaking stride as the cow also did in an attempt to confuse its pursuer. The horse's head bobbed, its mane flying out behind it, as it kept after the cow.

Gabe hung on to his hat as they went down into another more shallow draw, the dapple sliding down it and raising a cloud of dust as it did so. The cow ran along the bottom of the draw, its nostrils flaring and its ribs expanding as a result of its heavy breathing.

Sweat flew from the dapple's neck and struck Gabe in the face. Its saltiness stung his eyes. He grabbed the saddle horn with his free hand and gripped it tightly as the cow climbed up and out of the draw and the dapple climbed up right after it.

The dapple outdistanced the cow and promptly cut in front of it. The cow skidded to a dust-raising halt, its lower jaw dropping down until it almost touched its outstretched front legs.

My turn, Gabe thought. He leaned down from the saddle and hit the cow in the face with his slicker, which made a crackling sound as it struck its target. The cow's tail dropped. It blinked and then blinked again as Gabe struck it a second time with his slicker. Then it threw back its head and bawled. Gabe raised his slicker, ready to strike again, but the cow got up and ambled away, no longer running but still bawling.

The dapple walked almost sedately behind the cow as it drove the animal in the direction of the herd, which was bunched in the distance with two men riding slowly around it in opposite directions. Gabe gave his mount no guidance, taking pride in the fact that the dapple knew exactly what to do and how to do it.

They had almost reached the herd when the cow suddenly sprang to life and went racing to the right. Horse and rider went after it. The dapple neatly cut the animal off and turned it. As the cow tried to dash to the left, the dapple was there before it to nip the maneuver in the bud. The same thing happened when the cow lunged to the right again. Within minutes, the animal was back in the herd and Gabe was patting the neck of his horse and whispering words of congratulations to it on a job well done.

"Well, sir," Wes Harrison called out as he rode up and moved a bull he had brought back into the herd, "that cow sure did give you a run for your money."

"It did," Gabe readily admitted. "If it hadn't been for my horse, I'd still be chasing it. But he brought it to ground once I let him have his head."

"That's the thing about a good cutting horse," Wes declared. "It's often as not got more sense than the man aboard it."

Gabe sat tall and lean in his saddle and gazed out over the open land as Wes Harrison, softly whistling a lilting tune, did the same.

His face was lightly shadowed by the brim of his black slouch hat, but his features were nevertheless clear. His nose was narrow and straight and bisected two slightly sunken cheeks. His broad forehead showed faint traces of lines on it, and there were similar lines at the corners of his mouth. His lips were thin and could, when he was angry, set themselves in a grim, unsettling line. His gray eyes were keen and missed nothing. His long hair was the color of sand. It hid both his ears and the nape of his neck.

Despite his slender build, he had broad shoulders and a broad chest. His limbs were as lean and muscular as the rest of his body.

He wore clothes, dusty now from the roundup, which had seen better days. His jeans were worn at the knees and his boots were worn down at the heels. The felt band on his hat was frayed. But, despite the well-worn condition of his clothes, he presented an oddly dignified appearance which had something to do with the confident way he sat his saddle and with the clear steady gaze of his gray eyes which seemed to see straight through to the heart of whoever or whatever he looked at.

His cotton shirt was blue, and his leather vest was black. Around his neck was tied a red bandanna, and this one touch of color gave him a subtly jaunty air.

In the holster on his right hip, its butt forward to allow for a fast cross draw, hung a well-oiled Frontier Model Colt .44.

Beside him, Wes Harrison was a sharp contrast. Wes was a good foot shorter than his friend and built like a barrel. His face was slightly pudgy, and his fingers were thick and stubby. But many a man had been fooled by Wes's bulk and the air of casual indifference he displayed to the world. Wes could move with the swiftness of a striking snake and with the same deadly effect when the occasion called for it.

He wore a faded shirt that had once been brown and was now barely tan. His hat was a Stetson, also tan, with a curved brim. It had a ragged black-and-white feather tucked in its brim. His coarse twilled trousers were held up by a pair of braces from which a button was missing.

A .45 Smith and Wesson revolver hung holstered on his hip. The weapon's trigger guard had been cut away to allow for fast firing.

The tune Wes had been whistling died away. He pointed to a steer in the distance, which was standing half-in and half-out of some scrub. "Let's go git him, partner."

Both men spurred their horses and went galloping toward the steer, which stood almost casually watching them, seemingly unaware of the fact that they were about to make life difficult for him. But, as the two riders neared him, the steer swung his head and lumbered through the scrub, trampling some bushes and breaking off the branches of others.

Before they reached the scrub, the pair of riders parted, Gabe heading to the west, Wes to the east. They were circling around the scrub toward each other when the steer emerged from it.

"Ki-yi-yippay!" Wes shouted and headed straight for the steer.

It skidded to a halt, turned, and found itself facing an oncoming Gabe aboard his dapple, spinning his slicker above his head. The steer did not hesitate. It turned again and headed back into the relative security of the scrub.

Wes and Gabe exchanged glances, and then both men turned their mounts and headed into the scrub after their quarry. They chased it out of the meager cover and into the open where Gabe hazed it with his slicker and Wes, *ki-yi-yippaying* all the while, moved in close to the animal and used the great bulk of his horse's body to prod it along toward the herd in the distance.

For a short time the steer let itself be bullied along by Wes's horse and the sting of Gabe's slicker. But then, as if it had had enough of the men's rough treatment, it suddenly balked, bellowed, and lunged at Wes's big-barreled buckskin.

Wes, who had seen the move coming, managed to move his mount safely out of the way of the steer's potentially deadly horns.

The steer lunged again, making a 180 degree turn as it did so. This time the animal's left horn grazed Wes's horse, which let out a scream and would have reared in pain and fright if Wes had not kept it under strict control.

He backed his horse away from the steer while, on the animal's opposite side, Gabe did the same in order not to goad it into any further attempts to injure Wes or the horse he was riding.

"Maybe we can drive him in slow and easy from behind," Gabe yelled above the shouts of the other cowboys involved in the fall roundup.

Wes nodded and dropped back.

The steer stood its ground, its great head swinging from side to side, its small black eyes set in its white face swiveling from Gabe to Wes and back to Gabe again.

Gabe moved slowly forward toward the animal. So did Wes. Gabe raised his slicker.

The steer's head rose. Its eyes fastened on the slicker. As the garment began its swift decent, the steer backed up, and the slicker swished harmlessly through the air in front of its face. The steer bellowed angrily. It began to advance. One step, then another. Suddenly, it was running toward Wes, who had to turn his buckskin and move it and himself swiftly out of the animal's way.

Gabe, surprised by the steer's aggressive move was momentarily left behind.

Wes spurred his horse into a trot. Glancing over his shoulder and seeing the steer still on his back trail, he spurred the buckskin again, hard enough this time to leave cat tracks on its flanks, and went galloping away.

Gabe's eyes narrowed and his spine stiffened. He, too, put spurs to his horse and went after the steer, intending to cut it off before it could close in on Wes. He had to complete his maneuver before Wes reached the rim of the canyon that was directly ahead of him. He watched both steer and rider, waiting for Wes to turn. . . .

But Wes, with the steer on his buckskin's flying heels, seemed to be unaware of the danger directly ahead of him in his frantic hurry to escape the attack of the enraged steer.

"Wes!" Gabe yelled at the top of his voice. But Wes did not respond.

Too much noise, Gabe thought. The cowboys shouting, the clatter of hooves and horns, the bawling of cows. He can't hear me, Gabe thought, as he rode on, lashing his dapple with his reins to squeeze every ounce of speed he could from the animal.

He came up beside the steer, separated from it by no more than two yards. His intention was to cut between it and his friend, but he saw that there was no room to execute such a maneuver because there was less than two feet between the steer and the rump of Wes's buckskin.

"Wes!" he shouted again, even louder than the first time, as his dapple swung its head and bit the steer's flank, which had no effect on the animal. "*Wes!*"

Whether Wes had heard him or not, Gabe couldn't be sure. Perhaps as he neared the rim of the ridge, Wes realized the danger he was facing. In any event, Wes turned his horse at a right angle to the precipice in order to avoid going over it. But the turn was too sharp. The buckskin under him lost its balance and went down, throwing its rider into the path of the steer that was thundering toward him.

Gabe had no choice, and he knew it. So he did the only thing he could do. He aimed his horse at the steer and braced himself as well as he could for the collision that was coming. When it came, it sent horse, rider, and steer sprawling to one side, a huge jumble of hooves, horns, and flailing limbs.

Gabe hit the ground—no, not the ground, he realized, but the side of the downed steer. He thought his shoulder was going to break as a result of the impact. It didn't. His horse rolled over twice, stirrups and reins flying through the air, and then sprang to its feet. Gabe, from where he lay sprawled and stunned on the ground saw it shake its head in bewilderment, and then he was scrambling out of the loudly bawling steer's way so that he would not be crushed by the animal as it clumsily lumbered to its feet.

The steer then charged once again for Wes who, when he saw it coming at him, fled from it.

Gabe got to his knees as the steer began to close in on Wes and drew his gun. He cocked it and fired. Dust shot up directly in front of the steer where his round had buried itself in the ground as he had intended. The sound of the shot and the dust confused the steer. It turned and raced to the side—and over the edge of the ridge.

Gabe heard the loud impact of the steer's body hitting the rocks below.

As Wes staggered up to him, a chagrined Gabe shook his head. "They'll take that animal's price out of my pay, no doubt. I meant to scare him with that shot, all right, but I sure didn't mean to send him over the edge."

"If they dock your pay for what happened," Wes said, sucking in air, his chest heaving, "I'll pay you back half of whatever they take. What happened is as much my fault as it is yours."

He took off his hat and slapped it against his thigh to rid it of some of the dust that covered it. "I thought I was gone to glory for sure when that animal decided he was out to get me, which he damn near did. He scared the hell out of me, if you want to know the truth. He had a look in his eyes just like the Devil himself, red-hot from home!"

Gabe smiled. "Get your horse, and let's head back. We've still got us a bunch of cows to round up." He started walking toward his dapple. "I know a good place to find them, some of them, anyway. See that pole down there in that little valley?"

"I see it. Let's go!" Wes got his buckskin, swung into the saddle, and the two men rode out, heading for the tall pole, the top of which they could see sprouting in the distance. As they rode down into the shallow valley where it stood surrounded by cattle, they exchanged glances, and Wes said, "Look at that, will you? They're just waiting for us to come calling on them."

They rode up to the pole that was one of several the cowboys had scattered about the area. Each pole had been coated with salt and tallow to attract cows to what they considered a delicacy. There were seven head gathered around the pole now, all of them busily licking the salted tallow. Gabe and Wes rounded them up and moved them out.

On the way back to the main herd, they made, at Wes's suggestion, a short detour to a watering hole where they found nearly a dozen additional head placidly grazing the bluestem or settled down on the ground where they contentedly chewed their cuds. The two men rounded them up and drove the entire lot they had gathered back to where the herd was located.

As they approached their destination sometime later, they saw Buck Chandler, boss of the roundup, engaged in what appeared to be a heated conversation with a bearded man they both recognized, who was flanked by several of his outriders.

"That's Matt Lanier," Wes commented. "Now, I wonder what's got his dander up."

They soon found out as they rode up to the gathering.

"That calf—and those calves over there," Lanier was saying, "they're mine, and I mean to have them."

"I'm sorry to hear you say that, Mr. Lanier, sir," said an elaborately polite Buck Chandler, "because I can't let you have them."

"You can't—" Lanier spluttered, his face reddening in exasperation. "What the hell do you mean you can't let me have what's rightfully mine? Those calves—every last one of them—bear the brand of the Double Star— my brand. You can see that as plain as the nose on your face, Chandler."

Buck glanced at the calves in question. Then he glanced back at Lanier. "I see that those critters bear some kind of brand that might pass for yours. But there's another thing I also see, and that's the thing that makes me say you can't have them because, brand or no brand, they ain't yours."

"What the hell are you talking about, Chandler?" Lanier bellowed, his hands dropping to the butts of the two guns he was wearing.

"Look yonder, Mr. Lanier, sir," an unperturbed Buck said and pointed. "Look you how those calves are sucking those cows."

"What of it?"

"What of it?" Buck repeated, assuming an expression of utter surprise which would have done credit to the actor, Edwin Booth. "Why do you suppose they're doing that?"

"Doing what?" Lanier cried, his exasperation growing and his face becoming a deeper shade of red.

"Sucking our Rocking W cows," Buck replied.

"Because—well, because they're probably hungry, that's why," Chandler roared.

"Go on with you, Mr. Lanier," Buck said, a boyish grin and an "aw, shucks" expression on his face. "You're pulling my leg."

"I am not a humorous man, Chandler," Lanier snarled. "Now, me and my boys are going to take those calves that bear our brand back to our ranch and leave you and your men with a warning. Don't try rustling stock that bears the Double Star brand, or you'll find yourself in a whole lot of hot water."

"How long you been a cattleman, Mr. Lanier?" Buck asked innocently.

"Long enough."

"Maybe not long enough," Buck ventured. "I mean a cattlemen of some experience, why, he'd know right off when he saw a calf suckle a cow that the calf belonged to that cow, that she was that calf's mama. There ain't no surer way to tell who belongs to who in the cattle business than that, and I mean including brands on calves that somebody put there knowing that those calves weren't his to brand in the first place."

Gabe, watching the encounter and listening to the words just spoken, thought Lanier was about to explode.

The man's face went from red to white. His thick lips worked, but only spittle, not words, emerged from them. Gabe tried not to smile, but he was aware that Wes Harrison was grinning from ear to ear as he sat his saddle by his side.

"Boys," Lanier said to the men with him, "round up those calves and drive 'em back to our ranch where they belong."

"I wouldn't do that, gents, if I were you," Buck said calmly. He pointed to Gabe and Wes, to the guns they had drawn, which were leveled at Lanier and his Double Star hands.

"Buck's got a good point, Mr. Lanier," Gabe said evenly. "If you insist on trying to ride off with stock that's not yours, you might find the going tough. Hot lead in a man makes the going that way. It tends to weigh him down."

Lanier hesitated.

"You want we should shoot them down, boss?" the man standing next to Lanier asked.

The cattleman hesitated as Gabe raised the barrel of his gun and took aim at Lanier's head. Then, he said, "No, don't. We'll ride out. I don't want anybody to get hurt."

"Me neither, Mr. Lanier, sir," said a broadly smiling Buck Chandler. "I'm glad to see you've chosen to travel the sensible course in this little set-to we've been having here amongst ourselves. You all have yourselves a pleasant journey home, hear?"

Lanier muttered a colorful oath. But he and his men climbed aboard their horses, wheeled them around and rode out.

Gabe holstered his gun. So did Wes.

"Glad you boys rode up when you did," Buck told them. "Glad, too, that you used your powers of persuasion to send those cattle thieves packing."

"They might come back," Gabe commented. "With reinforcements."

"I don't think so," Buck mused, stroking his chin and watching Lanier and his riders vanish in the dust they were stirring up. "Lanier knows I had him dead to rights. He's not going to start a range war over a few calves. But if he does, well, we'll be ready for him."

"I'm ready for some grub," Wes said. "Has Cook got some to give us?"

"Go ask him," Buck said. "You're a bit early for supper, but go ask him. Although Clancy's not known to harbor a kindly heart where hungry cowboys are concerned, he just might let you have something to stop your guts from grumbling."

"Buck," Gabe said, "I had a run-in with a steer which ended up with—"

"Wait a minute," Wes said, interrupting his friend. "*We* had a run-in with a steer."

"Which ended up with," Gabe resumed, "the steer going over that ridge back there and killing himself."

"Gabe saved my life," Wes said. "That steer had spilling blood—mine—on his mind." He explained to Buck what had happened.

"That's nothing to fret over," Buck concluded when Wes had finished speaking. "No roundup ever covers he dog completely," he said. "A few head of stock always get away."

Gabe acknowledged the roundup boss's remarks with a grateful nod, and then he and Wes turned their horses and headed for the rope corral where the wrangler kept the drive's remuda.

The stamping and nickering of one of the horses in the remuda woke Gabe in the middle of the night. He lay there wrapped in his blanket, his hat, boots, and colt by his side, and stared up at the stars that shared the sky with the full moon. The night air was cool, almost cold, causing him to wrap his blanket more snugly about his body. He closed his eyes. He shifted position. He tried to ignore the soft snoring of a man sleeping not far away.

Sleep eluded him. The noises of the night, many of them unnoticeable by most white men, kept him awake. He found himself thinking of the Oglala Sioux, among whom he had spent his boyhood with his mother. She had been captured by the Indians in a bloody battle in which his father had been killed.

His mother had told him many times about that battle. She always spoke in hushed tones, and Gabe remembered her face as always being pale as she told him of what had happened before he had been born.

She and her husband, Adam Conrad, broke off from a wagon train bound for California and with about twenty other settlers headed for the Black Hills where, it was rumored, gold had been discovered.

"We'll find our fortune there, Amelia," Adam had promised his young bride. "I just know we will."

And so they rode up into the Black Hills in the Dakota Territory.

"It was a lovely cool morning in August," Gabe's mother would say, "when we arrived. Your father and I, we lay together in each other's arms that morning. . . ."

Gabe soon came to understand that it was on that morning that he had been conceived. It was on that morning, too, that the Oglala attacked the emigrant train that had invaded their favorite summer hunting grounds.

The battle, Amelia Conrad told her son, lasted for an hour. At times, it seemed that the Indians were winning; at other times, the emigrants seemed on the verge of routing the attacking Indians. She spoke of the terror that had possessed her during that long fight as she watched first one, then another and another of the wagon train's staunch defenders fall. But the final horror was yet to come. In time, it did come.

Amelia watched, overcome with fear, as Adam Conrad, her beloved, went down with a lance piercing his chest.

"My fear," she had told her son more than once, "gave way to fury when I realized that Adam, your father, was dead. I wanted revenge. I found a musket that one of the train's defenders had dropped, and I proceeded to pour powder down its barrel. I intended to fight in Adam's place. But a warrior came and tore the gun from my hands.

"Soon it was all over. The shooting stopped. No more lances or arrows flew through the air. I was taken prisoner and brought back to the Oglala camp where you were eventually born."

"Were you unhappy in those days?" Gabe would ask when he was old enough to fully understand the story his mother often told him.

"I was," Amelia admitted. "But I had to go on. I had to survive. For your sake, my son."

Gabe's thoughts drifted back to the present. Here I am, he thought, white by birth, Oglala by upbringing. How much of me, he wondered for the thousandth time, is Oglala and how much is white? Only an Oglala, he thought, would be able as I am now to hear the field mouse that is softly scurrying through the grass not far away. I feel more Oglala than white, he thought, I always have.

He had spent his first fourteen years with the Oglala, the People, and had become one of them. Now he lived with one foot in the Oglala world and the other in the white world.

Gabe smiled into the darkness as he recalled the old days, the good days of his youth lived among the People. Sometimes he yearned to return to those days, but he knew there was no going back.

An owl hooted somewhere in the darkness.

The moon sailed serenely in the sky.

Gabe waited patiently, and at last, like a shy woman, sleep came slowly and enfolded him in her dark arms.

CHAPTER TWO

The following morning, after the last of the cattle had been rounded up out of the scrub and the draws, Gabe, Wes Harrison, and the rest of the men began driving them down out of the hills to their home pasture where they would spend the winter.

Buck Chandler rode in front of the herd with Gabe and Wes riding point on either side of it and the other men occupying flank, swing, and drag positions.

The cattle moved without much trouble. Only occasionally did one of their number take a notion to go on a sight-seeing tour of its own, and when this happened one of the riders would go out after the animal and turn it back into the cut without too much trouble. Gabe, riding on the right of the herd, listened to Wes Harrison as he sang what seemed to be innumerable choruses of the popular tune, "Little Joe, the Wrangler." The music, if you could call it that—Wes had a voice that was both harsh and unable to carry a tune with any consistency—seemed to have a soothing effect on the cattle. They lowed, some of them, as they lumbered along,

warily noting the positions of the riders on either side
of them.

The drive halted when the sun reached its meridian.
The men made their nooning then, which consisted of
son-of-a-bitch stew, corn bread, and stewed tomatoes.
One by one as the men finished eating, they threw
whatever amount of coffee remained in their cups onto
the water barrel, as was the custom. When the coffee
evaporated it would help to cool the water contained in
the barrel, which would make drinking it pleasant in the
heat of the day.

In mid-afternoon, the sky darkened and rain began to
fall—rain that was accompanied by hailstones, some as
big as quail's eggs. The hailstones unsettled the cattle,
and the cowhands, wearing their slickers and with their
hats pulled down low on their foreheads, had to ride hard
to keep them from stampeding. As lightning flashed in
the sky, followed by the sound of thunder cannonading
across the land, they had their work cut out for them.
The cows' lowing gave way to a nervous bawling. But
Gabe, Wes, and the rest of the cowhands managed to
contain the herd, and when the rain stopped at around
four o'clock, the men breathed sighs of relief and began
to relax.

That night Buck Chandler called a halt at a corral
owned by a Texas rancher he knew. He negotiated with
the man over the price of renting the corral for the night
and, when the haggling was through, Gabe and the others drove the herd into the corral and closed the gates.
The men fell asleep that night to the sound of lowing,
contented cattle as the stock settled on their bed ground

behind the poles of the corral, their temporary home.

In the morning, after a breakfast of kidney beans and salt pork, they repeated the previous day's routine, throwing the herd on the trail just after the sun had dried the heavy coating of dew that covered the grass.

Chandler had refused to move out any sooner, pointing out that the wet grass would soften the hooves of the cattle and turn some of them into cripples before they got where they were going.

The sun was well on its way down to the horizon that day when the Rocking W Ranch came into sight in the distance. As Gabe, Wes, and the other men drove the cattle across the tableland to what would become their winter range, a middle-aged man came out of the ranch house and stood watching the proceedings.

While his men worked the cattle, Chandler, rode up to the house and spoke to the man, whose name was Charles Everhard. He was the owner of the Rocking W.

The conversation was brief. When it was finished, Chandler headed for the bunkhouse where his men had gone. Once inside it, he slammed the door behind him and stood there not saying anything for some time.

Gabe watched him. He saw the tension in Chandler's face. He saw the way his eyes avoided direct contact with the eyes of any of the men. Something was wrong. Chandler was normally an open and friendly man who never stood on ceremony. A man whose cowhands were as much his friends as they were paid ranch hands.

Gabe glanced at Wes, who rolled his eyes as if to say he, too, had seen what Gabe had seen written on Chandler's face and was preparing himself for the worst.

"I just had a talk with Mr. Everhard," Chandler said at last, still not looking directly at any of the men in the bunkhouse. "I guess you all know what's coming, boys."

No one spoke. All the men waited for Chandler to go on.

"Winter's on its way," Chandler said. "It'll be here before we know it. Mr. Everhard won't be needing as many hands come winter as he does the other three seasons of the year."

There were murmurs among the men.

"He's going to have to let you go, boys," Chandler said, staring at the floor. "He can make do with his year-round hands until spring rolls around again. He told me to tell you that you're all welcome to come back next year. He told me to tell you that you've all done a fine job and he appreciates it. He'll welcome you back, each and every one of you, he said, with open arms. Well, I guess that's it," Chandler concluded.

"I swear," said a man named Chick Landers, "I don't know why I stick to cowboying. It's only worth forty a month and found, and more often than not I'm out of a job and down on my luck."

"There's always riding the grub line to look forward to, Chick," someone said.

"Not me. I don't take handouts. I'd sooner starve than let anybody give me charity."

"I guess I'll head on home to my wife," a man known only as Mooch muttered. "I can't stand the old woman, but at least she feeds me when times turn tough."

"Well, Gabe," Wes said, "what do we do now?"

Gabe shrugged. "Move on. There's nothing else we can do."

"Move on where?"

Gabe didn't answer for a moment. "One place is about as good as another, I reckon."

"It's going to be hard finding a job to get us through the winter," Wes said. "Maybe we should head down into Mexico. At least it'll be warm down there, and we won't freeze to death."

"But we might starve to death down there. There's no work to speak of. I say let's head up across the border."

"Into Indian Territory? That's rough country up there. It's chock-full of bandits and all kinds of other riff-raff."

"Maybe we can hire on to help keep the peace in one of the towns up there."

"Sounds good to me."

"Then come morning we'll draw the pay that's due us," Gabe said, "and ride north."

Gabe and Wes got an early start the next day. They left the Rocking W Ranch behind them and rode north. The early morning air was alive with bird singing. The sun was just above the horizon and was already turning the prairie golden as they rode across it. Hummocks here and there cast shadows, and low ridges bisected the blue sky in places. There was a feeling of peace about the land, and in Gabe's mind there was also a feeling of anticipation. He didn't know what he was anticipating, not specifically. In a general sense, he supposed, he was anticipating the future and what it might hold for him.

"We've got a long ride ahead of us," Wes said. "What say we stop over in Denton? Denton's a nice town. It's usually full of Texas cowboys, and that means there's usually a fight a minute in the only saloon in town. It's called the Alhambra, by the way."

"I know. I've been to Denton a time or two. That was before I had the misfortune to hook up with you."

"Misfortune? I'll tell you something, my friend. The day you hooked up with me was the luckiest day of your formerly sorry life. I've gotten you out of more hot water and nasty scrapes than I could begin to shake a stick at. Why, were it not for me, you'd probably be cooling your heels in some Texas jail right this very minute. Or maybe you would have stretched a rope with that scrawny neck of yours. You're a brawler—"

"Only in self-defense."

"—and a womanizer."

"Only when I'm lonely."

"That combination is a recipe for trouble."

"You're speaking, of course, from long and bitter experience."

Wes gave Gabe a look of mock annoyance. Then he spoiled the calculated effect by grinning from ear to ear. "I do, and that's a sad and sorry fact. I've been in more barroom brawls and whorehouse beds in my time than a man twice as smart as me could count."

"Which leaves you with a lot of memories."

"You're right on that score. Some good, some bad. Now there was a working woman I had the misfortune to meet up with, name of Gap-tooth Alice, up in Abilene last year. That was before I met up with you. She and I hit it off real fine—at first. She invited me—did I ever tell you about Gap-tooth Alice and me, Gabe?"

"Only about a million times."

Wes fell silent and pretended to sulk.

"Speaking of working women—"

Wes immediately brightened.

"—they have a few in Denton, as I recollect."

"And every one of them's a comfort to a man's body, if not to his immortal soul."

"Maybe we can dally with a couple of them before tonight's over."

"I think that's much more than just a maybe, knowing you and me," Wes said.

Gabe laughed, startling a roadrunner which went racing, tail up, across their trail.

The Alhambra Saloon was noisy, crowded, smoky, and filled with an assortment of what Wes, at one point, called "soiled doves."

Gabe had his eye on one dove who had red hair, green eyes, and a curvaceous body that kindled his desire.

When she noticed Gabe watching her, she elbowed her way through the crowd of drinkers and cardplayers toward him.

"I haven't seen you in here before, stranger," she said as she took up a position beside him at the oak bar.

"I can say the same for you," he told her. The scent of lemon verbena she wore tickled his nostrils.

"I just got into town a week ago. I used to be a hostess in a saloon down in Nogales. I wouldn't object if you offered to buy me a drink."

Gabe summoned the bar dog, and the woman ordered brandy.

"I'll see you later back at the hotel," Wes told Gabe, giving him a lascivious wink. "I'm going over to talk to that sweet-faced and sweeter-assed blond-haired lady over there in the corner."

"Which of us gets to use the bed in the room we rented over in the hotel?" Gabe asked him under his breath. "You or me?"

"I'll flip you for it." Wes pulled a coin from his pocket. "Call it."

"Tails."

Wes flipped the coin. "Sorry, old son. Heads."

When Wes had gone, Gabe turned to the woman he had been talking to and said, "You live in town, do you?"

"I have a room in the hotel, yes."

Ah, he thought. The problem of where to spend the night with his companion was solved.

"My name's Gabe," he volunteered.

"You can call me Cindy."

"I could also, in all honesty, call you pretty."

Cindy smiled and placed the tip of her right index finger on Gabe's chin. "You're sweet."

"I'm also horny." No sense beating around the bush, he figured.

"I can see that." Cindy's eyes dropped then she looked up at him again. "I really don't want another drink. Shall we go?"

Arm in arm, they went.

Once inside Cindy's room with the door closed, she put her arm around Gabe's neck. She drew him down toward her and kissed him passionately on the lips.

"What's your pleasure, Gabe?" she asked coyly.

He told her in no uncertain terms.

She smiled and led him to the bed that filled most of the small room.

When he arrived back in the Alhambra Saloon, Gabe looked around to see if Wes Harrison was there. When he didn't spot him, he took a seat near the door.

He had not been in the saloon more than five minutes before a disturbance erupted at the bar. From where he sat, he could see a veritable mountain of a man arguing vehemently with a man standing next to him. The man who was doing all the talking—shouting, actually—was tall and brawny, with shoulders as wide as an oxen yoke and arms and legs like the trunks of trees. He had a face that was dominated by bushy eyebrows as black as his piggish little eyes that were set deep in his skull. His lips were full and seemed to flap as he spoke—roared. He sported a full black beard that seemed to bristle as he raged on at his abjectly cowed companion, who was trying to back away from him.

But every time the much smaller man did so, the loudmouthed man reached out, seized him by his coat's lapels, and pulled him back into place.

A man got up from a table and went up to the big man who was gripping the lapels of the other man as he shouted obscenities at him.

Since the saloon had fallen unnaturally silent as its patrons warily watched the encounter between the two men, Gabe was able to hear most of the conversation that ensued.

"Archie," said the man who had been seated at a table, "why don't you just settle down and stop all this jabbering?"

Archie never even looked at the man who had just spoken to him. But he answered the man's question with a snapped, "Mind your own goddamned business, Lester!"

"He's going to hurt me," the man caught in Archie's clutches cried to the man named Lester. "Please, sir, don't let him hurt me!"

"Archie, leave him be," Lester said in a firm voice. "Let's you and me belly up to the bar, and I'll buy you a drink."

"This ain't none of your affair, Lester," Archie barked. "Now get away from me—*far* away!"

Lester reached out and clapped a hand on Archie's shoulder.

A mistake.

Archie, without turning his head or so much as looking at Lester, swung his arm and struck Lester with it, sending the man staggering backward as if he had just been poleaxed.

Shaking his head in dismay as he recovered his balance, Lester returned to his table muttering, "Well enough's best left alone."

"Fight, you little sissy!" Archie loudly challenged the man whose lapels he was crushing in his huge hands.

"I don't want to fight!" the man shrieked in terror.

"I told you he was a sissy!" Archie shouted to no one in particular.

"Please, Mr. Hoover," the man pleaded, "just let me go. I'll leave, and I won't bother you anymore. I'm sorry if something I said upset you. I'll—"

"You'll go all right!" Archie Hoover roared. He spun the man around, seized him by the collar and the seat of his pants, carried him the length of the bar, and then threw him bodily through the batwings, smashing them to smithereens as he did so.

Outside, the thrown man scrambled to his feet. Holding his bloody head in both trembling hands, he ran without stopping until he had disappeared from sight.

Dusting his hands and wearing a smug expression on his beefy face, Archie Hoover strode across the floor and took up his former position at the bar. He held up his empty glass and yelled, "Fill 'er up!" at the bar dog, who obediently hastened to do exactly that.

"Don't you move," Hoover ordered the bar dog. He downed his drink and held out his empty glass.

When the bar dog had refilled it, he promptly emptied it again.

A shrill whistle caused Gabe to turn his attention from Hoover to the saloon's entrance. Wes Harrison stood there just beyond the broken batwings, whistling through his teeth, both hands on his hips as he surveyed the extensive damage.

Then he sidled into the saloon, carefully avoiding the shards of broken wood hanging from bent hinges. When he saw Gabe, he gave him a smart salute and sat down at the table next to him. "What the hell happened?" he asked, jerking a thumb over his shoulder at the remains of the shattered batwings. "Were you in an all-fired hurry to get back inside here? Is that what happened to the batwings?"

"*He* happened to them," Gabe answered, indicating Archie Hoover with a nod of his head.

"Big bastard, ain't he though?" Wes leaned across the table toward Gabe and, grinning, said, "I had me the time of my life just now. That woman—she calls herself Fancy and, by God, she is that—knew more positions than six acrobats, I swear, Gabe. And some of them, had you told me about them, I would have sworn weren't humanly possible. She had me up and she had me down and she twisted me sideways until I didn't know where the hell I was at. But what I did know was she made me feel like I never felt before. And I'm talking about from head to toe and all the way back again. But there's always a worm in the apple somewheres, sad to say."

"What do you mean? You just said she gave you the time of your life."

"After it was all over I was lying on the bed as naked as a jaybird with my eyes shut and feeling close to falling asleep. That's when I heard Fancy pussyfooting around the room.

" 'What're you doing, honey?' I asked her.

" 'Oh, nothing,' she says. 'Just getting dressed.'

" 'Wait,' I says. 'I'll get dressed and go back to the saloon with you.'

"I sat up on the bed and, lo and behold, there she was with her hand in a pocket of my jeans. She got my poke out and was tucking it in her garter when I bounded off the bed and grabbed her and took my money back faster'n a stuttering man can say shucks. Then I gave Miss Fancy the bum's rush."

Wes assumed a mournful expression as he propped his chin in his hands and stared across the room toward the bar. Dreamily, he said, "I swear, I always have bad luck where women are concerned, Gabe. They either try to steal my money or don't measure up to my dreams. Either way, I wind up a loser. Someday I hope I'll meet up with a woman who's sweet and thinks the world of me, and we can get married and raise a family.

"I'm sick to death of consorting with soiled doves. I want a good woman. One I can respect and love and work hard for. You know, Gabe, I laugh and joke and so on, but deep down I'm a lonely man. I never fessed up to that before but, by God, it's the truth. But how's a fiddle-footed man like me ever going to meet up with a decent woman when I live my life on the run from here to there without never a minute to stop and catch my breath?"

"Maybe you ought to quit the trail, Wes," Gabe suggested. "Like right now. Denton's a nice town. You could get a job here, and I'll wager that you'll be in love with a decent woman and she'll have you hitched, bridled, and saddled before you know what hit you."

Wes smiled. "Maybe I should do that. Maybe I will." He paused a moment and then shook his head. "I'm fooling myself again. I have to be on the go, Gabe. I have to find out what's around the bend in the crick and over the mountain. I'm a cursed man, is what it amounts to, I reckon."

Gabe's attention was diverted from his friend to the man named Archie Hoover, who was striding across the room toward their table.

"What do you think, Gabe? Do you think I'm condemned to wander for all the rest of my born days?" Wes asked plaintively.

Gabe, his attention focused on the approaching Archie Hoover, didn't hear the question.

"Gabe?"

"Here comes trouble," Gabe said.

Hoover arrived at their table. Speaking to Wes, he asked, "What do you think you're looking at, mister?"

"What?" Wes asked, only then becoming aware of Hoover's presence at the table. "What are you talking about?"

"You were staring at me, that's what I'm talking about."

"Me? I wasn't staring at you," a baffled Wes said. "I was just—"

"On your way, Hoover," Gabe interrupted. "My friend and I don't want company."

Hoover ignored Gabe and spoke again to Wes. "Maybe you didn't like what you were looking at, is that it?"

Wes smiled. "Mister, I don't want any trouble. If I seemed to be staring at you—well, I'm sorry. The fact is I wasn't. But I'll apologize anyway if that's what you want, and we'll let bygones be bygones."

"Why, you sniveling little son of a bitch!" Hoover muttered. He reached out and seized Wes in both hands and dragged him to his feet, almost knocking over the table as he did so.

Wes's smile faded. A look of cold fury swept over his face.

Gabe shot to his feet. "Take your hands off him," he ordered Hoover.

"You got to stand in line, cowboy," Hoover muttered. "When I'm through wiping the floor with your girlfriend here, I'll start in on you."

Gabe's fists rose.

But before he could deliver a blow, Wes told him, "I'll handle this, Gabe. You step back out of harm's way, hear?"

Gabe protested, but Wes ignored him, so he stepped back as Hoover let go of Wes and swung a roundhouse right.

The blow landed on Wes's left shoulder and caused him to stumble to one side. But he immediately regained his balance and headed for Hoover, his fists raised and clenched so tightly his knuckles were white. Head down, he moved in on Hoover and then let fly with both fists almost simultaneously. His left landed on Hoover's jaw and his right slammed into Hoover's chest.

Hoover grunted and noisily sucked air into his lungs. With his eyes glued on Wes's face, he raised a hand and gingerly moved his jaw from side to side.

"Let's go, Wes," Gabe said during the pause in the fight. "Let's get out of here now while the getting's good."

Wes shook his head. "This fella wants to fuss, well, I'll fuss with him, and when we're through he'll wish he'd never laid eyes on me."

Hoover thrust out his right fist which landed squarely on Wes's nose, almost breaking it. Blood flowed from his nostrils, which Wes wiped away with the back of one fisted hand. Then he threw a left uppercut which caught Hoover under the jaw, snapping his teeth together.

Someone in the saloon let out a cheer in appreciation of the telling blow Wes had delivered. Someone else applauded.

The cheer and applause enraged Hoover. He hunched his head down and came at Wes swinging. Wes danced backward on the balls of his feet. He ducked a blow Hoover threw at him and circled his opponent, taunting him with mocking laughter instead of words.

Hoover's rage intensified. That rage was apparent in his rabid eyes and in the pugnacious set of his jaw as he went after Wes, who continued circling and dancing, keeping just out of reach of Hoover's deadly fists.

Finding his opponent as elusive as a butterfly, Hoover let out a furious roar and lunged at Wes. Before Wes could fend him off, Hoover had Wes in a tight grip, his arms encircling him. He squeezed, and the air gushed out of Wes's harshly compressed lungs.

Hoover brought one knee up and slammed it savagely into Wes's groin.

As Wes let out a cracked cry of pain, Gabe, angered at Hoover's tactics, reached out and grabbed him by the neck. He squeezed hard, forcing Hoover to release Wes.

The instant Hoover's hands fell away from Wes, they were both turned on Gabe. Pummeling Gabe with both fists, Hoover dropped him to his knees. Gabe fought his way to his feet under a flurry of Hoover's blows, most of which landed on the top of his head, and swung.

His left uppercut sent Hoover flying backward to crash into a table, splintering it and sending poker chips scattering across the floor.

Hoover reached down and picked up a splintered length of wood from the broken table. Swinging it from side to side, he advanced on Gabe, who quickly backed away but suddenly found himself with his back to the wall.

He tried to duck under the wooden weapon Hoover was wielding, but it connected with his skull and sent him spinning down into a deeper darkness than any he had ever known before.

CHAPTER THREE

Consciousness returned slowly to Gabe. With it came a throbbing pain in his head which seemed capable of exploding his skull. When he opened his eyes, the lamplight in the saloon blinded him. He shut them again and only then became aware of the shouting and hooting that filled the room. Cautiously, he opened his eyes again, giving them time to adjust to the relative brightness of the saloon.

The fight was continuing, its spectators placing bets with one another and jeering or cheering their choice as blow after blow continued to be struck by both fighters.

Gabe winced, not because of his own pain, but at the sight of Wes. The man's face was bloodied so that his left eye was all but hidden from sight. Blood had dripped onto his clothes, and the knuckles of both his hands were skinned and also dripping blood.

Gabe winced again as he saw Archie Hoover trying to brain Wes with the piece of wood he still had in his hand after having used it to such devastating effect on Gabe himself.

But Wes swung his head to one side and tilted his body at a nearly forty-five degree angle so that the weapon in Hoover's hand went over his head and did no damage. Wes butted Hoover with his head, driving the man back into the wall where Wes held him as he delivered a flurry of blows consisting mainly of well-aimed one-two punches into Hoover's fleshy gut.

Hoover slid down the wall. For a moment he sat, dazed, on the floor. As he shook his head, sweat flew from his face to spatter nearby spectators. Groggily, he got up again and went for Wes with the piece of wood in his hand.

Wes kicked out at him and succeeded in sending the wooden weapon flying across the room and out of Hoover's reach. His friend was weakening, Gabe could see. The fact that Hoover had a good thirty pounds on him was one of the reasons. Another was the fact that Hoover apparently possessed the stubborn stamina of a full-grown grizzly bear. Hooking his thumbs, Hoover moved forward, reaching for Wes's eyes, obviously intending to gouge them out of his head.

Wes deflected the attempt by throwing up his arms and knocking both of Hoover's arms aside.

Gabe struggled to his feet. He reached out and held on to a green, baize-covered table to help steady himself and then, when he thought he could remain upright if he moved, he advanced on the battlers circling one another in the middle of the saloon. He had to make his way toward them through the treacherous litter of broken tables and chairs which covered the floor.

Hoover saw him coming. He turned from Wes and went for him.

Gabe threw a punch that caught Hoover squarely on the jaw, causing him to gag. He followed up with a savage series of body blows.

Hoover, still gagging, swung his left arm. His fist crashed into the side of Gabe's head. Gabe lost his footing on the wooden debris littering the floor and, before he could regain it, Hoover took advantage of his unsteadiness and pummeled him mercilessly. Gabe seized Hoover by the shoulders and arms and tried to hold him at bay. But Hoover broke Gabe's grip and continued to attack him.

Hoover grunted as Wes leapt into the air and landed on his back. Wes's arms went around Hoover's throat, and he began to choke the life out of the much larger man.

"Two on one!" somebody yelled. "That's not fair fighting!"

"Two of us make one of him!" Wes yelled to counter the criticism as he held on to Hoover for dear life.

Hoover spun in a circle, roaring now, as he tried to dislodge Wes from his back. When he could not do so, he turned and ran backward.

Wes screamed as Hoover slammed him against the bar. His hands gave way, and he fell to the floor.

Gabe lunged at Hoover, reaching for the man, wanting to throttle him. But he never got a hold on him. Hoover bent down, picked up a broken table leg, and brained him with it.

He went down, the darkness returning once again. But before it could drown him, he saw with horror that Hoover had drawn a knife from somewhere and was advancing on Wes, who lay stunned on the floor, blood blinding him as he tried to rise.

Gabe saw Hoover haul Wes to his feet with one meaty hand and plunge the knife into Wes's gut with the other. Then he lost consciousness again.

Someone was after him. Gabe ran, but the man pursuing him ran faster. Gabe dodged in among some trees and then came out of them and found himself in a town. Behind him the man now had a knife in his hand, a long knife with a double blade. The wicked instrument glinted as it caught the light of the sun, which turned it a bright blood-red.

Gabe ran on and then, finding no refuge anywhere, turned and stood his ground, prepared to fight the man with the knife until one of them was dead. But with his bare hands? He looked down at them and wished he had a weapon, any kind of weapon.

Then the man was upon him, and he was trying desperately to fight him off while at the same time trying to wrest the knife from his hands. He failed on both scores. He saw the knife in the man's hand rise. Nothing else existed in the world for him but the knife and the hand that held it. He was paralyzed. He discovered to his dismay that he couldn't move so much as a single muscle. All he could do was stare up at the knife and watch its slow descent as it made its awful journey down toward his chest. . . .

Consciousness abruptly returned to Gabe. The man in his deadly dream vanished. So did the knife the man had been holding. He found himself lying on the floor of the Alhambra Saloon. Not far away was a crowd of men, their backs turned toward him. He propped himself up on his elbows and groggily shook his head. Pain tore through it. He sat up and then slowly got to his feet. What had happened? At first, he couldn't remember. Then, gradually, it all began to come back to him. There had been a fight. A fight between Wes Harrison and Archie Hoover.

The knife!

Gabe remembered seeing it just before he sank into unconsciousness—remembered seeing it slice its way into Wes's gut. He groaned and made his way toward the phalanx of backs facing him.

He shouldered his way through the crowd and then halted and stared down at the two men on the floor. One was lying on his back—Wes Harrison, his eyes staring at the ceiling. The other, a man with a doctor's bag, was down on one knee beside him. He shook his head and looked up at the circle of faces.

"He's dead," the doctor said. He closed his bag and stood up. "He doesn't need me. He needs an undertaker. Who did this to him?"

"Archie Hoover," Gabe said flatly, still staring down at the corpse of his friend.

"Archie Hoover," the doctor repeated. "It figures. He's killed more men than the law can count. Why'd he do it?"

"He picked a fight with my friend," Gabe said dully. "He said Wes was staring at him."

"He had a mite too much to drink," the bar dog with the sleeve garters said, shaking his head as he stared at Wes's body. "Archie's bad enough when he's sober as Sunday, but drunk as a deacon, why, he's pure hell on the hoof."

"So's his older brother, Oren," someone volunteered. "They outdo each other where hell-raising's concerned. That Oren's as mean as a cat with its tail caught in a crack."

"A fact," someone else agreed. "You all remember the time Oren took a fancy to Mrs. Cosgrove here in town?"

There were nods and murmurs of assent from the other men.

"He went after her hammer and tongs, and never mind that she was married and her man was still alive and kicking. Oren didn't let a little thing like that stand in his way. When the lady would have no truck with him because, as she told him in no uncertain terms, she was a virtuous married woman, he solved that problem—to his satisfaction, at any rate—by shooting Bart Cosgrove down like a dog and claiming it was self-defense. Then he went to Bart's missus and told her she was free to be with him. He never could understand why she still wouldn't have anything to do with him."

"Or why she went and hanged herself the day after her man was planted," someone else said softly. "Oren thought she should have welcomed him with open arms with her man dead and gone."

"It's kind of hard to fathom," a man in the crowd mused. "Oren and Archie's daddy, old Caleb Hoover, is a religious man from the very git-go. Always spoutin' Bible verses and calling souls to salvation. How he could have sired two such tomcats as Archie and Oren is way beyond me."

"They're a close-knit family, though, I've got to say that for them. Ever since Mrs. Hoover died of the galloping consumption, the three men she left behind her have stuck together and fought each other's battles without so much as a flinch or faintness of heart. I suppose you could call that Christian brotherhood of a sort, though I don't hold with killing and raping and plundering as the three Hoovers are wont to do when the notion strikes them."

"Where is Hoover?" Gabe asked, having seen no sign of the man since he regained consciousness.

"Archie's long gone, mister," one of the men in the crowd told him. "He lit a shuck right after he stuck your friend."

"Before the law could get here and lay hands on him," another man volunteered. "He's wanted dead or alive as it is for killing a woman up in Notch Hollow after raping her. I'm surprised he had the nerve to show himself in town like he did, what with the price he's got on his head."

"Five hundred dollars," the doctor said thoughtfully. "I wouldn't go out after Archie Hoover if the bounty was as high as five *thousand* dollars. The man's as likely to kill you as look at you."

"Where might I be likely to find him?" Gabe asked, his gaze shifting from one man in the crowd to the next.

"I saw him ride out after he ran the hell out of here," one of the members of the crowd declared. "He headed due west."

"Doc," Gabe said, "my name's Gabe Conrad. I'd like to arrange to bury my friend before I ride out after Hoover."

"Mr. Conrad, I know you feel bad about what happened to your friend," the doctor said, "but I think a word of warning is warranted here and now. Let the law handle Hoover. He's bad medicine, believe me."

"Real bad medicine," the man standing next to Gabe emphasized.

"A word to the wise, they say, is sufficient," the doctor declared with a sage nod directed at Gabe.

"Where can I find the undertaker?" Gabe asked.

The doctor pointed to a sallow-faced man wearing a black suit, boiled white shirt, and a black string tie. "That's Mel Cutter. He's our undertaker and coroner."

"I shall be pleased to be of assistance to you, sir, in this, your hour of sad need," Cutter said mellifluously.

"How much?" Gabe asked him bluntly.

"Well, our basic coffin—made of solid pine, mind you—costs—"

"How much for the whole thing, coffin and burying both?" Gabe asked.

Cutter quoted a price, and Gabe promptly paid it. Then he turned on his heels and left the saloon. He made his way to the livery where he and Wes had left their horses when they arrived in Denton. He sold Wes's horse and gear to the farrier there, then paid his boarding bill and rode out of Denton, heading west after Archie Hoover.

Gabe rode into the setting sun, his eyes on the trail he had found and was following at a trot. The hoofprints he was sure belonged to Hoover's horse were clearly outlined in the soft ground, which meant that Hoover was making no effort to hide his trail. Apparently he was not in any particular fear of pursuit.

He thinks he cowed me back there in Denton when he did in Wes, Gabe thought. That I won't come after him.

That nobody will, the law included. He's a confident fella, this Archie Hoover. Well, we'll see how confident he turns out to be if and when he spots me riding his back trail.

He rode on across a savannah that was covered with lush grama grass and then up a hill that rolled like an ocean wave up out of the flatland. From its crest, he surveyed the countryside below him. There was a stand of cottonwoods growing on the bank of a stream that ambled along down below him. The timber, he noted, was thick enough to hide a man and a horse.

Gabe dropped back below the ridge line in order not to skyline himself. He dismounted and climbed the hill, where he bellied down on the ground to watch the area below. He thought there was a good chance that he might spot Hoover down below. There was water if Hoover or his horse, or both of them, were thirsty. There was wood if Hoover had it in mind to build himself a fire to brighten the night that was coming.

He waited, watching.

Less than ten minutes later, he saw tendrils of smoke rising above the trees. The smoke hadn't been dissipated by the branches of the cottonwoods, which meant that Hoover—if it was his fire burning out of sight down below—was in a clearing or camped on the bank of the stream.

Leaving his horse hitched to the ground behind him, Gabe made his way down the hill, crouching and keeping his head down as he went. He moved on as the sun sank below a distant range of mountains, turning the sky above the mountains first a bloody orange and then a deep purple. As he came closer to the grove of cottonwoods, he could smell the smoke.

When he reached the timber, he moved stealthily in among the trees, drawing his Colt as he did so. Keeping his thumb on his gun's hammer, he moved closer to the crackling sound of the fire he could hear but still not see, burning up ahead of him. Moments later, the fire—and Archie Hoover, who was hunkered down beside it—came into view. A feeling of intense satisfaction swept over Gabe, but he set it aside, concentrating instead on the task at hand, which was to get the drop on Hoover.

He moved forward. But despite his cautious approach, he stepped on a dry piece of wood that had broken off a deadfall.

The sound of the wood snapping caused Hoover to rise and quickly turn. "Damnation!" he exclaimed, reaching for his holstered gun. "You!"

"Me," Gabe said. "Don't draw. You do, you're dead."

Hoover's hand froze halfway to his gun as he glared at Gabe, the crackling of his fire the only sound in the otherwise quiet evening.

"Drop your gun and get on your horse, Hoover," Gabe ordered, nodding in the direction of the buckskin that was browsing the bark of one of the younger cottonwoods in the grove.

"What's this all about?" Hoover asked, as he tossed his gun to the ground.

"You know damn well what it's all about," Gabe snapped, picking up Hoover's gun and thrusting it into his waistband. "It's about my friend back in Denton—my friend you killed. That's what it's all about. Now move, mister, or I'll drill you right here and now."

Hoover's eyes never left Gabe's implacable face. "Where we going?" he asked, without so much as blinking.

"Back to Denton. I'm turning you over to the law there. I hear they want to get their hands on you. I hear you're wanted dead or alive for raping and murdering a woman in a place called Notch Hollow."

"Mister, you're making a big mistake. You do me wrong, and I got relatives—friends, too—who'll make you regret what you say you're fixing to do. We Hoovers stick together. Some say we're clannish. Well, I say that's a good thing and one to be commended. So why don't you just turn yourself right around and ride off, before you do something you're sure to be sorry for."

"Get on your horse," Gabe ordered peremptorily.

Hoover started to say something but then apparently changed his mind. He moved slowly toward his buckskin, warily watching Gabe as he did so. When he reached his horse, he stepped into the saddle and snarled, "What now?"

"Now we head up that hill back there," Gabe told him. "You first. I'll be right behind you, so don't try anything. If you do, I'll drop you. Now, move out."

Hoover meekly obeyed the order. Moments later, he was riding up the hill with Gabe walking briskly behind him. Both men were halfway up the hill when Hoover suddenly reached down and came up with a hide-out gun, a single-shot derringer he had withdrawn from his boot. In one swift movement, he turned and fired at Gabe, knocking Gabe's gun out of his hand with his well-aimed shot. Then he was galloping up the hill and, a moment later, down its other side.

Cursing, Gabe retrieved his gun and raced up the hill. When he crested it, he found that Hoover was already far away—and leading Gabe's dapple as he made good his escape. Hoover's mocking laughter drifted back to him. He swore again and went racing down the hill in what he recognized as a vain attempt to recapture Hoover. He fired at the man, but Hoover was already well out of range of his side arm. He ran on, trying desperately to shorten the distance that separated him from Hoover, but the effort was useless. The distance gradually lengthened until he could no longer hear Hoover's laughter. Minutes later, he could no longer see the man, who had disappeared around a bend in the dark distance.

Gabe skidded to a halt, frustration fueling the fury that was growing within him. I had him, he thought. I had him, and I let him get the drop on me. He swore under his breath and began to lope along as he continued his pursuit of the man who had murdered his friend.

He knew the odds of catching his quarry were against him. But he was determined to play the cards he had been dealt. He increased his pace, but finally slowed and came to a halt as the moon rose to join the silver stars in the black sky above him. Even with the moon's white light, he knew he could not trail Hoover in the dark. What's more, he thought, the bastard just might be up ahead there somewhere, waiting to ambush me in the dark. He could shoot me down before I even knew he was within firing distance of me.

He decided to spend the night right where he was. In the morning, he would set out again after Hoover.

• • •

Gabe resumed his pursuit of Hoover in the gray light of the next day's false dawn. The man's trail wasn't hot, but it hadn't grown completely cold either. Gabe loped across savannahs rich with grass and up and down rocky hummocks as he relentlessly continued his pursuit. He trailed Hoover into a stream and, by scanning the streambed for traces of horses' hooves in the sandy bottom that the current had not yet completely obliterated, he found the place where Hoover had left the stream and returned to dry ground.

Hoover was heading back toward Denton now, Gabe realized. He quickened his pace until he was running as fast as he could. He ignored his hunger. He had no time for hunger. He had time only for Hoover—and revenge. Once he had recaptured the man, there would be time enough to satisfy his hunger.

He came to a gorge and followed Hoover's trail down into it. Now why, he wondered, as he tracked his quarry through the deep draw, didn't Hoover just ride around this gulch? Why would he bother coming down into it when he could just as easily have detoured around it with a lot less trouble? The questions made him uneasy.

He moved on, more slowly, his eyes on the tracks he was following. He stopped and looked back over his shoulder, his hand dropping to his gun butt. A draw was a great place for an ambush. Let your prey enter it, then one man moves into it behind him. Another one pops up at the far end of the draw. They both move toward him. They start shooting. . . .

But there was no sign of anyone behind him. Besides which, Hoover was on his own. He had no confederate

siding him. At least not as far as Gabe knew, so there
should be no ambush down here in the draw.

He looked up and saw a wide strip of sky above him,
framed by the two benches on either side of the draw
above him. Sunlight slanted down into the gulch but did
not reach its floor, where it was shadowy and still except
for the sound of Gabe's footsteps.

He had almost reached the end of the gulch when he
thought he heard a sound from above him. He looked up,
but saw no one. He waited a moment, listening, his eyes
raised, and then moved on. Behind him, a pebble rolled
down the steeply sloping right side of the canyon from
the bench above.

He turned, his hand going for his gun. Above him a
horse nickered. He looked up, his gun clearing leather—
and saw Archie Hoover fly through the air and come
hurtling downward toward him.

Before he could even cock the hammer of his gun,
Hoover landed on top of him. The air gusted out of
Gabe's lungs as he was knocked down to the ground.
His gun fell from his hand. As he tried to turn, tried
to reach for the weapon, Hoover, grinning the grin of
a demon just released from hell, hit him on the side
of the head with a rock he had picked up from the
canyon floor.

Pain and bright red light flashed through Gabe's skull.
The pain made him cry out, a wordless wail, and the red
light blinded him.

He felt rather than saw Hoover rip his own gun,
which Gabe had taken from the killer earlier, out of
his waistband. He grabbed for it, unable to see where
it was, and his fingers closed frustratingly on only air.

Sight returned to him just as Hoover, using his gun's barrel as a kind of small crowbar, placed it against Gabe's throat and then, gripping the weapon with both hands, began to make a seesaw motion with it.

Gabe gagged. The unyielding and merciless metal cut off his air and made his throat burn. He seized Hoover's wrists and tried to pull his hands away, but they remained steadfastly where they were. So did the gun barrel, which was threatening at any moment to shatter Gabe's windpipe. He gagged again.

And brought his knees up. . . .

They slammed into Hoover's buttocks, forcing the man forward and causing him to lose his grip on his gun. The instant the gun was no longer choking him to death, Gabe slammed both palms against Hoover's chest and threw the man over his head. As Hoover flew through the air, Gabe scrambled to his feet. He reached down and grabbed Hoover by the back of the neck. He hauled the man to his feet, spun him around, and sent his left fist plowing into the man's face.

Blood spurted from Hoover's split lower lip. He coughed and a piece of one of his teeth flew from his mouth. Letting out a vicious roar, he made a grab for Gabe, but Gabe sidestepped, kicked him in the groin, and then pounded him brutally with both fists. As Hoover slumped to his knees, Gabe scooped up Hoover's gun which lay on the ground by his boots. The derringer had been knocked far away from them. He also drew his own gun. He stood there then, feet planted far apart, both guns cocked, his chest heaving as he tried to catch his breath and waited for Hoover to recover.

Hoover looked up at him through bleary eyes. "I'm going to kill you!" he muttered through clenched teeth.

"With what? Your bare hands?"

Hoover's eyes dropped to the guns in Gabe's hands.

"Get up," Gabe ordered. "Get up, you ambushing son of a bitch, before I blow your head off!"

Hoover struggled slowly to his feet.

"The horses—mine and yours—you've got 'em up on the bench?"

Hoover nodded.

"I take it you saw me coming on your back trail?"

Hoover nodded again. "If I'd have had that gun you took off me back in the woods, I'd have plugged you before you even went down into this draw. As it was, I had to jump you from up on the bench. I didn't want to get a bullet in the back."

"I'm no back-shooter."

"So you say."

"Let's go," Gabe said. "Up to the bench. We're riding out for Denton, you and me."

Hoover glumly turned and, holding his hands high, began to make his way through the draw with Gabe following closely behind him.

"You know, it's going to be your word against mine," Hoover said over his shoulder. "Nobody who was in the Alhambra'll say that I killed your friend."

An incredulous Gabe said, "They all—or most of them, I reckon—saw you do it, the same as me."

Hoover left the draw and started to climb up to the bench. "They'll keep their mouths shut. They know better than to go up against a Hoover. They know that if they do, all the Hoovers will be after them. That's something I tried to tell you before. You're asking for trouble bucking the Hoover clan, mister."

"It won't be the first time I've bucked trouble," Gabe responded with equanimity. "Probably not the last either."

When they reached the bench, they made their way to where Hoover's buckskin and Gabe's dapple were quietly browsing.

"Climb aboard," Gabe ordered his captive.

Hoover put one hand on his saddle horn and a foot in the stirrups. He swung into the saddle and then, as Gabe was about to do the same, he jerked his reins as hard as he could, causing his horse to scream as the Spanish bit tore into the flesh of its mouth and drew blood.

The buckskin responded instantaneously by rearing in an effort to ease the pressure of the iron bit. Its front legs flailed the air.

Gabe tried to duck, but it all happened so fast that he didn't have a chance to do so. On its way down, the buckskin's right front hoof struck Gabe a crushing blow on the left shoulder, downing him and causing him to drop the guns in his hands.

Hoover swiftly slid out of the saddle and pounced on the guns before Gabe could recover from the brutal blow he had just received from the man's horse.

There was a smile on Hoover's face as he straightened up, both guns—his own and Gabe's—firmly in his hands, and said, "Looks like the tables have turned, mister."

The last word was barely out of his mouth when he fired off a pair of rounds. One of them tore into Gabe's upper right thigh, bringing piercing pain with it. As the round struck him, Gabe was bowled over.

Hoover walked toward him, twirling the guns in his hands. "I'm going to shoot you to death," he announced, still grinning. "But slow and easy. First I'm going to shoot you in the other leg. Then in the arms. One after the other. Then in the gut. Then in the chest. I'm going to fill you so full of holes you can be used for a sieve when I'm through with you."

Gabe forced himself to wait until Hoover had come closer to him. Then he acted. His hands closed on some of the deadwood's debris. He threw it in Hoover's face. Before the debris had even struck the man, Gabe was up on his feet and stumbling, because of his wounded leg, toward Hoover. When he reached him, he grabbed both of the guns in Hoover's hands and held tightly to their cylinders.

"*Goddamn* you!" Hoover screeched, trying to fire the weapons but unable to do so because Gabe's firm grip kept the cylinders from turning.

Gabe raised one booted foot and stomped hard on Hoover's left instep.

The man cried out in pain.

Gabe stomped his right instep even harder.

In his pain Hoover let go of the guns, which had been Gabe's goal.

Gabe tossed both guns into the air and caught them by their butts. When Hoover lunged at him, seized his right wrist, and twisted it to make him drop the gun he was holding in that hand, he succeeded only in forcing Gabe to fire that gun unintentionally.

The round ripped into Hoover's chest. Hoover staggered backward, an expression of utter dismay on his face. He looked down at the round red hole in his chest and then up at Gabe. He reached out with both hands in what appeared to Gabe to be an oddly pleading gesture. His knees buckled. He dropped down on them. Then he pitched forward on his face directly in front of Gabe's dusty boots.

CHAPTER FOUR

Gabe stood looking down at the lifeless body of Archie Hoover, a man he hadn't meant to kill, but a man whose death he did not regret.

For you, Wes, he thought. A life for a life. Blood for blood.

He could take the body back to the law, he thought, but then immediately dismissed the notion. He had no intention of trying to collect the bounty riding on Hoover's head. It had not been the money he wanted, but simply justice. All that mattered was that he had trailed his man, found him, and killed him. It was over now, ended. Wes was avenged.

Gabe dropped Hoover's gun on the ground and holstered his own. He bent over to examine the wound in his right thigh. It throbbed, but the pain was not that great. He could see the small hole the round had made. He found no place where the round had left his leg. So it was still in him somewhere. He would have to dig it out to prevent infection. He didn't relish the prospect, but he knew it had to be done. But not here, not now.

Not in the presence of Hoover's corpse. He wanted to get away from that ugly sight, which reminded him of what had happened to Wes Harrison.

He limped over to Hoover's buckskin. He stripped the gear from it and dropped the gear on the ground. Then he slapped the horse on the rump and it went racing away.

Then he went to his dapple, which tossed its head at his approach. "Hello again, old fella," he said softly as he stroked its smooth neck. "We're back together again, you and me," he said as he gently extracted a cocklebur from his mount's mane.

He looped the horse's reins over its head, stepped into the saddle, and moved out, heading north toward the Nations. He never looked back at the body lying on the ground behind him.

When he had traveled a few miles, he spotted a swiftly running stream and rode closer to it, hoping.

The stream's surface was covered with a thick growth of green watercress. Gabe's gut grumbled as he stepped down from the saddle and hunkered down on the bank of the stream. As he scooped up some of the dripping cress in his hand, his dapple lowered its head to drink noisily.

He broke off some of the glossy dark green leaves and began to eat them. He surveyed the stream in both directions as far as he could see, but there was no sign of any poisonous water hemlock, which also grew in running water. He ate until his gut no longer grumbled and his hunger was appeased.

Then he gathered some wood and started a small fire, which he would need for what he had to do next.

He pulled off his boots and then stepped out of his jeans. He sat down on the ground and blew on the kindling. When the fire was going strong, he drew his knife and held the blade in the fire for several minutes, then withdrew it.

Gritting his teeth, he probed his wound with the tip of his knife's blade. Pain shot through his leg. But he kept at it. Probing, digging. The blood began to gush from his leg. He ignored it. But he couldn't ignore the intense pain he was causing himself.

But the bullet had to come out, and he was the only one who could get it out, and this was the only way to get it out. An inch of the blade disappeared into his leg. Blood spattered the rest of it. Then the tip of the blade struck something. Gabe twisted the knife slowly. He felt the bullet move. He tilted the knife to one side to try to pry the bullet up and out. The tactic worked. The bullet burst out of his thigh.

Gabe rose and limped into the stream to wash away as much blood as he could. Then, back on dry ground again, he sat down next to the fire and placed the blade of his knife in the flames. He held it there as his blood, which covered the lower half of the blade, sizzled and popped.

When the blade began to glow pink and then red, he withdrew it from the flames. With his free hand, he thumbed a round out of his cartridge belt and placed it between his teeth. Biting down hard on the bullet, he forced himself to lower the knife and place it, flat side down, against the ragged and bloody wound in his thigh to cauterize it. His teeth almost lost their hold on the bullet as a scream of agony welled up in his throat, fighting to be released. But his teeth bore down on the bullet as the smell of his own burning flesh filled his nostrils. Then, he withdrew the blade. Charred bits of flesh came away with it.

He felt a giddiness wash over him, and for a moment he thought he was going to faint. The world around him flickered in and out of focus. He swayed and almost fell. But then the giddiness, and the dizziness that had come after it, faded away. The world steadied, and he knew it was over, that it was good to have endured.

The soreness in his shoulder from Hoover's horse having struck him now seemed like nothing compared to the searing pain in his thigh. He gingerly got to his feet and stood there a moment as a ghost of the giddiness he had felt earlier returned. But it soon passed, and he pulled on his jeans, buttoned them, and then sat down again and pulled on his boots.

He looked around him. There was water. Wood to feed the fire he had built. The sun was going down. He decided to spend the night where he was.

He slept until the sun was halfway to its meridian the next day. He ate some more watercress, then drank some water from the stream and filled his canteen with it. After stamping out the remains of his fire, he went to where he had picketed his horse for the night and tore up some grass, with which he rubbed the animal down. He checked its hooves and then saddled and bridled the animal. After carefully tightening his cinch, he flipped his stirrups down and climbed aboard the dapple.

That afternoon he reached the southern bank of the Red River. He rode along it, looking for a safe place to ford, where there was none of the treacherous quicksand for which the river was notorious. When he found a satisfactory spot, he walked his dapple into the water, and they made the crossing without incident.

Two days later, he rode into the town of Tishomingo in Chickasaw Nation. He stopped at a clapboard building that bore a sign: EATS. Leaving his dapple at the hitch rail out front, he went inside and ordered a meal that could easily have fed two men: boiled potatoes, a huge beefsteak, bacon, four fried eggs, and a pot of coffee.

His mouth watered as the meal was set in front of him some time later. He ate as if he were starved and within a matter of mere minutes, the meal had been completely devoured. He poured himself a cup of coffee and drank it as a sense of contentment settled over him.

When the waiter asked him if he wanted dessert, he ordered apple pie with vanilla ice cream and asked the man for the name of a good hotel in town.

"The Central's the best," the waiter answered without a moment's hesitation. "It's the only one in town that don't rent rooms to Injuns."

"Is that a fact?"

The waiter, seeing the stony stare Gabe was giving him, hurriedly turned and went to get the dessert his customer had ordered.

Later, when Gabe left the restaurant, he freed his mount from the hitch rail and led it to the livery that was just down the street. He left it there with orders to grain the horse and water him. Then he made his way to the Central Hotel, following the directions the waiter in the restaurant had given him.

When he reached his destination, he entered the four-story building and went up to the desk clerk. He rented a room, paying in advance as requested, and climbed the stairs to the third floor where he found his assigned room—number eleven—at the end of a dark hall. He unlocked the door and went inside.

He flopped down on the bed and sank into its sagging mattress. He folded his hands behind his head and thought of what the waiter had told him when he asked the man to recommend a good hotel.

"The Central's the best," the man had said. "It's the only one in town that don't rent rooms to Injuns."

And yet, he thought, here I am in Chickasaw Nation, which is run by and for the Chickasaw, and that white waiter is here only through the sufferance of the Chickasaw tribe. Strange are the ways of such white men. They are intruders in a land that is not theirs and yet they look with contempt—even hatred—on the native peoples.

I wonder what that desk clerk would think, he asked himself as he lay staring at the whitewashed ceiling, if he knew I'm as much an Oglala as I am a white man. Maybe more Oglala than white, when you come right down to it. To hell with him! Him and all the others whose prejudice blocked the trails the native peoples had to follow and whose guns often took the lives of those very same people.

A soft knock sounded on the door.

Gabe sat up, swinging his legs over the side of the bed. He drew his gun and took up a position next to the door, his back flat against the wall. Then he threw the door open.

"Oh, my!" exclaimed the attractive woman who stood outside in the hall as she faced him and the gun in his hand, which was aimed directly at her.

"I'm sorry," he said, flustered. "I didn't know who it was."

"It's just little old me," she said. "My name's Pearl."

"Mine's—"

"I know what it is. It's Gabe Conrad. I saw the register. The desk clerk is a friend of mine. Well, not exactly a friend. You could say we're sort of business partners. He told me you were here and suggested I stop by and pay you a visit. What he didn't tell me is that you're a good-looking fella."

Gabe stared at the woman, his smile returning. She was young—twenty, maybe twenty-two. Her blond hair was curled, and her figure seemed to have been poured into the short, red silk dress she was wearing. Her full breasts were revealed by her low-cut bodice. Her hips were also full, and her waist was tiny. She had long slender legs, and her blue eyes never seemed to stop twinkling.

So she'd come to pay him a visit, had she? So she was business partners with the desk clerk downstairs, was she? It all spelled sex to him.

"Come on in," he invited, holstering his gun and stepping away from the door.

She entered the room, but didn't bother to look around, which suggested to Gabe that she had probably been in this room or others like it in the hotel more than once. On business.

"I'm glad you asked me in," Pearl said. "I take it you have cash money to pay me with."

Gabe nodded.

"Then we might as well get down to business, don't you think?"

Gabe definitely thought so. He went to Pearl and put his arms around her.

"Why don't you get rid of this?" she asked, patting his revolver. "Guns make me nervous."

He unbuckled his cartridge belt and draped it over the back of a wooden chair.

Then she put her arms around his neck and kissed him with clearly professional passion.

As their kiss continued, she slipped out of her dress.

Later, they were both lying side by side on the bed, holding hands, when the door to the room flung open and a burly man with a full black beard burst into the room.

He stood there, his eyes wild and his lips working wordlessly, as he stared at them. His fists clenched at his sides as he finally found his voice and bellowed, "Bitch! I looked all over town for you. The desk clerk told me you were up here."

Pearl sat up, terror in her eyes, and began to pummel Gabe on the chest, screaming lustily as she did so.

"What the hell—" a startled Gabe cried as he rolled out from under her unexpected attack. He leapt to his feet and shouted over the sound of Pearl's continuing screams, "Who are you?"

"I'm Jerry Rutledge!" the man in the doorway bellowed. "And that there woman's my wife!"

Gabe glanced at Pearl, who began to weep. Through the hands she had raised to cover her face, she sobbed,

"He attacked me, Jerry. I was minding my own business outside the hotel, and he came along and grabbed me. He said he'd kill me if I made a sound. Jerry, I was so frightened, I didn't know what to do. He forced me to come up here with him and then—and then—"

"You say he attacked you?" Rutledge asked, frowning.

Pearl's hands flew away from her face, and she nodded vigorously.

Rutledge drew the gun that hung holstered on his hip. "Mister, I'm going to kill you," he told Gabe through clenched teeth. "Get set to die."

"Don't kill him, Jerry," Pearl pleaded as she jumped out of bed and slipped her dress over her head. "Let's just get out of here. I don't ever want to see that horrible man again." She pointed a trembling finger at Gabe.

Gabe lunged for his gun belt, which he had draped over the chair in the room. He never got to it. Rutledge stepped in front of him, cutting him off. Gabe stood there, naked and feeling completely vulnerable, and stared at the black hole in the barrel of Rutledge's gun, which was aimed at his head.

"Look, Rutledge," he said in a placating tone, "it's not like your wife said. I didn't rape her. She—"

"He *did*!" Pearl sobbed as she sat down on the edge of the bed and put on her shoes.

Gabe backed away as Rutledge took a step toward him. He found himself backed up against the bed as Rutledge continued advancing toward him.

"What's all the shouting about?" asked a man who appeared wide-eyed in the open doorway.

Another man and a woman appeared behind him. They stood there ogling the trio in the room, the woman paying particular attention to Gabe.

"Somebody better fetch the law," Gabe said, without taking his eyes off the menacing Rutledge. "This man's fixing to drill me."

"I'll get the deputy marshal," the man who had first arrived on the scene declared and promptly disappeared.

Rutledge's finger tightened on the trigger. He fired a round at Gabe, but Gabe ducked and the shot went over his head.

In the doorway, the woman screamed. The man with her gasped. Then they both fled.

As Gabe came up, he grabbed a pillow from the bed and thrust the pillow against the gun in Rutledge's hand. At the same time, he pushed the weapon to one side.

The gun went off again, ripping through the pillow and sending a flurry of goose down fluttering up into the air.

Gabe dropped the pillow, which had caught fire from the shot Rutledge had sent flying through it. He grabbed a porcelain pitcher sitting beside a basin on the dresser and doused the flames with the water it contained. Then he threw the pitcher. It struck Rutledge on the left shoulder.

Rutledge roared and, in a rage, raised his gun again.

Gabe threw himself to one side as Rutledge's gun roared. He collided with the chair and smashed it as he went down. He came up with his gun in his hand as Rutledge took aim at him again. Before Rutledge could fire again, Gabe did. His shot caught Rutledge in the gut and slammed him backward against the wall.

"You killed my man!" Pearl breathed, her voice almost inaudible. "You killed him *dead*!"

Gabe warily watched Rutledge for signs of life. He saw none. He put down his gun and pulled on his pants. He was buttoning them when two men appeared in the doorway. One was the man who had volunteered to go and get the law, and the other was a man who wore a nickel badge pinned on his leather vest. The badge bore the legend: United States Deputy Marshal.

"Don't move!" the deputy ordered, drawing his Smith and Wesson .44 and aiming it at Gabe.

"He killed my husband!" Pearl cried, pointing to Rutledge's corpse.

"What happened here?" the deputy asked, his gun never wavering.

"Rutledge burst in here—" Gabe began.

"And he *shot* him!" Pearl cried, pointing at Gabe.

"It was self-defense," Gabe insisted. He hurriedly explained what had happened.

"Arrest him, Deputy," Pearl cried. "Take him into custody. He's made me a widow!"

"Let's go," the deputy said to Gabe.

"Where?" Gabe muttered, pretty sure he knew the answer to the question.

"I'm taking you back to Fort Smith with me. You'll have to stand trial there before Judge Isaac Parker."

"Judge Parker," Gabe repeated in a monotone. "The Hanging Judge?"

The deputy nodded. "That's what folk call him. He's got jurisdiction over Indian Territory, unless the crime in question's been committed by one Indian against another. In that case, local tribal law takes over. Let's go," the deputy repeated sternly, gesturing with his gun.

"You mind if I finish dressing first?" Gabe asked. Without waiting for an answer, he proceeded to do just that. Then he handed his gun and gun belt over to the deputy and let himself be marched out of the room.

Behind him, he heard Pearl wailing.

Outside the hotel, he asked, "What about my horse? I've got him at the livery."

"We'll pick him up on the way," the deputy said.

They stopped at the livery where Gabe got his horse and gear and then rode out beside the deputy. When they reached the outskirts of town, Gabe looked around and said, "I thought you were taking me to jail."

"There's no jail in town. I've got my own. It's just around the bend up there."

When they rounded the bend, Gabe saw the "jail" the deputy had referred to. It was a wagon with barred sides and a barred top, a cage on wheels. There were two men in the cage, both of them with shackled hands and feet.

"You'll stay here tonight," the deputy said. "I'm expecting another deputy to show up in the morning. He'll drive the wagon back to Fort Smith."

When the deputy dismounted, Gabe did the same. The lawman marched him over to the wagon, unlocked the door at its rear, and Gabe climbed inside to join the other two prisoners.

The iron door clanged shut behind him. The deputy turned a key in its lock and then, after tying Gabe's horse to the rear of the wagon, walked away.

"Howdy," Gabe said to his fellow prisoners as he sat down on the bench that ran along one side of the wagon. "My name's Gabe."

The two men seated on the bench on the opposite side of the wagon said nothing for a moment. Then, one of them said, "I'm Rusty, and this here's Charlie."

"What'd you do, Gabe?" Charlie asked.

"I shot a man."

"You'll swing," Rusty remarked laconically. "Judge Parker's dead set against murder."

"It wasn't murder," Gabe said firmly. "It was self-defense. The man I shot was trying hard to kill me."

"You can prove that?" asked Charlie.

"I can tell my side of the story."

"Were there any witnesses?" Rusty asked.

"Yes. The man's wife saw what happened, only she lied and said—it's a long story and one I don't want to go into just now."

"They'll summon her to testify," Charlie said. "She'll see to it that you hang. Her and Judge Parker will."

Without consciously realizing what he was doing, Gabe put his hand on his throat.

Just after dawn the next morning, the deputy built a fire and proceeded to cook a greasy mixture of salt pork and kidney beans over it. When the stew was ready, he unlocked the barred door of the wagon and beckoned.

Gabe rose from the floor where he had been sleeping and took a step toward the open door at the same time that Rusty did.

"Not you," the deputy told him. "One at a time. Today it's Rusty's turn to eat first. Then Charlie's. Yours is last."

As Rusty stepped down from the wagon, his shackles clanging noisily, Gabe sat down on one of the benches and hung his head. He was hungry and thirsty, and he was also angry. Angry at the way events had developed and at himself for having let himself get into the situation he was in.

But it's not your fault, he told himself, as Charlie awoke, scratched, yawned, and took up a position on the other bench. It was just bad luck; you were with the wrong woman in the wrong place at the wrong time.

"Watcha got cookin', Deputy?" Charlie called out between yawns. "It smells like it needs a bath." Charlie's cracked laughter filled the air. "That deputy may be some kind of lawman, but he can't cook worth a tinker's damn," he told Gabe.

Gabe made no comment as he thought of what he might do to get himself out of the mess he was in. He was still deep in thought some ten minutes later when the deputy escorted Rusty back into the lockup and let Charlie leave it.

"Garbage," Rusty muttered under his breath when the deputy was out of hearing. "Back home in Tennessee, we wouldn't swill our hogs with that shit the deputy calls stew."

"I've heard it said that beggers can't be choosers. I reckon that goes for prisoners, too."

"I wish I could get out of here before we get to Fort Smith," Rusty remarked dolefully. "If I don't, I'm a dead man for sure."

Gabe waited for the man to elaborate.

"Charlie and me, we robbed a stage. Killed the driver and a passenger. We're sure to hang if we ever get to go before Judge Parker. Do you think the three of us could get the drop on that other deputy that's supposed to put in an appearance today to cart us to Arkansas?"

"That's exactly what I've been thinking about," Gabe said. "Three against one. Those are pretty good odds, I'd say."

"But Charlie and me, we got these." Rusty indicated the shackles binding both his hands and feet.

"You could choke the breath out of a man if you wrapped those shackles you're wearing on your wrists around his neck and pulled them nice and tight."

Rusty smiled. "You could, by golly, you sure as hell could." His face fell. "But these deputies, they all got guns."

"But we've got brains," Gabe said.

They both turned to the east when a shot sounded somewhere off in that direction.

"Hunter, maybe," Rusty speculated. "Out early after some breakfast."

Gabe glanced at Charlie, who was hunkered down in front of the deputy's cook fire, forking food into his mouth like a starving man. He wished Charlie would hurry up and finish so that he could get out and get something to eat. His gaze shifted to the deputy, who was standing some distance from the fire, his gun at the ready as he watched his prisoner eat.

"Somebody's coming," Gabe commented a moment later.

Rusty looked around. "I don't see nobody."

"Neither do I. But I heard a horse."

"You've got keen ears then. I don't hear a thing."

"There," Gabe said, nodding toward the man who was riding toward them from the southeast.

"That fellow's built as solid as a four-seater out-house," Rusty observed. "He's tall, too. Not a man to tangle with, I'd say."

Gabe had to agree with Rusty's evaluation. As the man came closer and Gabe could make out his ebony eyes, he saw in them a coldness that chilled him. They were the eyes of a snake as it glides toward its prey. But he was smiling. Somehow his smile did not warm the look in those disturbing eyes of his.

Out of the corner of his eye, Gabe saw the deputy thumb back the hammer of his gun.

"Back inside," the lawman ordered Charlie.

"But I ain't finished eating yet," the prisoner protested.

"Shut your mouth and do like you're told," the deputy barked.

Grumbling, Charlie put down his plate and headed for the wagon with the deputy right behind him. He was safely locked inside with Gabe and Rusty when the stranger rode up and gave the deputy a cheerful greeting.

"I see you are about the law's important business," the man told the deputy with a wave of his arm in the direction of the wagon and the three prisoners penned inside it. "It's a reassuring sight to see, Deputy."

The lawman said nothing. His gun was aimed directly at the new arrival.

"I wonder if you have any vittles you can spare a hungry traveler, Deputy?"

"Help yourself. Stew's still hot."

The stranger, dressed all in black, got out of the saddle and went to the fire. He picked up the long-handled spoon from the stew pot and ladled up some of the mixture. After tasting it, he smacked his lips appreciatively and served himself.

The deputy watched him eat. After some time had passed, he holstered his gun.

"What about *my* breakfast?" Gabe called out from the portable jail.

"You'll get yours when our visitor's finished his and is on his way again," the deputy responded, with a meaningful glance at the stranger.

The man cleaned his plate and set it down on the ground. His hands moved swiftly, fluidly, as he drew his guns and trained them both on the deputy.

CHAPTER FIVE

"Don't go for your gun, Deputy," the man with the two guns in his hands said. "I've got the drop on you, and I'd just as soon kill you as I killed that other deputy I ran into a ways back, who said he was on his way here to rendezvous with you."

The deputy's jaw dropped. "You killed Sam Crawford?"

"I killed a deputy, yes. I didn't ask his name."

"But—why?"

"I have business here, and I didn't want him around to interfere with it. You alone I can handle easy."

"Business?" the deputy repeated. "What business do you have with me?"

"Not with you exactly, Deputy. With one of your prisoners."

The deputy's eyes flicked to the three men who were all standing and clutching the bars of the wagon as they watched and listened to what was taking place. Then his gaze returned to the stony face of the man with the guns in his hands.

"Which one?" the deputy asked.

"That one."

Gabe realized that the man had pointed one of his gun barrels directly at him. He frowned. This all made no sense to him. He didn't know the man, had never even seen him before—at least, not as far as he could recall.

"Let him loose, Deputy," the gunman ordered.

"See here, now. I've got a duty to perform. I can't release any of my prisoners."

"Damn you and your duty, lawdog!" the man cried, his voice rising to a keen pitch that made Gabe's ears ring. "Let him loose and do it now!"

Biting his lower lip, the deputy moved slowly and reluctantly toward the wagon, pulling a ring of keys from his pocket as he went. When he reached his destination, he glanced back over his shoulder at the gunman.

"Do it, Deputy," the man ordered.

The lawman did.

In a moment, Gabe was out of the wagon and standing on the ground a few feet away from the deputy.

"What about us, mister?" Rusty called through the bars to the gunman. "You're not going to leave us to languish in here, are you? Let us out, too, while you're at it."

The gunman was silent.

"It won't be any skin off your ass," Charlie called out to him. "So what do you say? Will you get us out of this cage, too?"

The gunman ignored both men. "Get on board your horse," he ordered Gabe, indicating the dapple.

Gabe freed his horse from the rear of the wagon and swung into the saddle. He waited for whatever was about to happen next.

The gunman fired the gun he held in his right hand.

The round struck the deputy, who spun around and fell heavily to the ground.

"Hey!" Rusty yelled as the gunman and Gabe turned to leave. "You can't leave us caged up in here like this! Not with the deputy dead, you can't! We'll starve to death!"

The gunman swung around in the saddle and fired a warning shot in the direction of the wagon. "Keep still," he told Rusty and Charlie. "Don't open your mouths, either one of you, till we're well away from here. You got that?"

"Yes, sir," Charlie said.

"Yes, sir," Rusty echoed, "we've got that. We won't say so much as a single word."

"If I hear a peep out of either one of you," the gunman said solemnly, "I'll ride right back here and finish you both off. That's a promise. It'll be as easy as shooting fish in a barrel."

Gabe said, "That deputy back there, he's got my gun."

"You won't be needing your gun," he was told.

"A man out here in Indian Territory without a gun's in big trouble," he argued, but fell silent as the gunman raised the pistol in his right hand.

"Shut up!" the gunman snarled.

Gabe decided he had no choice but to play along for the time being with whatever the man wanted, since he held all the high cards at the moment.

"Got a question for you," Gabe said as they rode on.

His companion gave him a sidelong glance.

"When that deputy back there let me out of the cage, you told me to climb aboard my horse. Now what's been gnawing at me ever since is—how did you know this here dapple belonged to me?"

"We'll stop up ahead," the gunman said, indicating the edge of a canyon. "As for your question, maybe this will answer it. My name is Oren Hoover."

Gabe stiffened. "Oren Hoover," he repeated. "You're Archie Hoover's kin?"

"His older brother."

They drew rein not far from the edge of the canyon.

"Telling me your name doesn't really answer the question I put to you just now," Gabe said.

"I've been hunting you," Hoover said. "When Archie didn't show up where and when he was supposed to meet me and our pa, we waited a spell and then we went looking for him. In Denton, we found out that he'd had a set-to with a friend of yours, which led to your friend getting himself killed. Folk there told us your name and said you'd set out after Archie to get even. They said you rode west after him. On a dapple."

"Got it," Gabe said warily.

"Folk in Denton, when pa and me asked them what you looked like, told us, so when I caught up with you back there in that deputy's custody I knew right off who you were."

"You said you and your pa were in Denton together. How come he's not here with you now?"

"He stayed put. He sent me to find Archie and warn him you were after him. But I was too late. You got to my brother before I could."

"You found him?"

"What was left of him after the buzzards had gotten through with him. *You could have at least buried him after you killed him!*" Hoover screamed, losing control.

"It wasn't a cold-blooded killing like you're probably thinking," Gabe stated. "He had two guns, one of them mine. We fought. One of the guns went off and killed him."

"It don't make no never mind to me what happened. All I know and all I want to know is that you went after Archie intending to do him in and, by God, you did!"

"Now you're fixing to do the same for me."

"You got that right. I'm going to kill you, Conrad. I most surely am going to do that."

"How come you didn't do it back at the wagon?"

"Couple of reasons. One, I didn't want to have to worry about trying to kill you while holding that deputy at bay. Two—and this one's important—I passed this spot while I was trailing you and figured it would be a good place to do the deed my way."

"Your way?"

"My *special* way. Get down off your horse, Conrad." Gabe dismounted.

"Walk over yonder." Hoover gestured toward the rim of the canyon.

Gabe hesitated a moment, his eyes boring into Hoover's and then slowly walked toward the rim of the canyon. When he reached it, he turned and looked back at Hoover.

"Jump," Hoover said.

"*Jump?*"

"Down into the canyon."

Gabe turned his head and gazed down into the canyon. He was looking at a drop of several hundred feet. He was also looking at a jagged jumble of rocks that littered the floor of the canyon. He glanced back at Hoover. Slowly, he shook his head.

"You won't jump?"

Gabe shook his head a second time.

"Well, now, maybe I can persuade you to do like you're told. Yep, I think maybe I can do that."

Hoover cocked his gun. He fired. The round bit into the ground barely a foot in front of Gabe's boots, kicking up dust.

Gabe held his ground, but he could feel himself starting to sweat.

Hoover drew back the hammer of his gun again. He squeezed off a second shot, which whined past Gabe's right ear.

"I'm a fair man," Hoover said, with an edge of sarcasm in his tone. "I'm giving you a choice of how you'll die. By jumping or getting your hide filled full of holes. Now I ask you, Conrad, what could be more fair than that?"

When Gabe said nothing, Hoover added, "My brother was on the verge of getting married, did you know that? True. He had a nice girl all picked out and primed. A bit of a hellcat, but Archie liked his women and horses spirited. You ruined her life, Conrad. Just like you took Archie's. Now you have to pay the price for what you did.

"We Hoovers, we take care of our own. That means even after death. Like I'm doing right now for Archie. He'd do the selfsame thing for me, I've no doubt about it. The dead can't seek vengeance. But the living can do it for them. That's a thing we Hoovers have always believed. And the woman Archie was fixing to hitch up with, she feels the same way, almost as if she was a Hoover born and bred. Now are you going to jump, or am I going to put a hole in your heart?"

Gabe tensed as he watched Hoover's finger grip the trigger and slowly tighten on it. He wanted to go after the man, but the distance between them was too great. If he tried that, he would be dead before he had traveled ten feet.

Hoover's next shot grazed Gabe's neck, drawing blood.

The shock of the shot striking him unbalanced Gabe. He staggered backward and then, realizing his precarious position on the canyon's rim, stepped swiftly forward again. But an instant too late. The ground beneath him gave way as a result of his weight pressing down upon it. He fell backward—and went over the rim.

He flung his arms out, his fingers grasping. His legs were below the rim and then so was his pelvis. As his torso slid downward, his fingers managed to close on a rock formation jutting out from the edge of the rim. He gripped it tightly with both hands and hung on, his boots scrabbling for a foothold on the wall of the canyon.

He finally found a toehold. Thrusting his right boot into it, he stayed perfectly still for a moment as gravel dislodged from the rocky outcropping showered down upon his head. He squeezed his eyes shut and held on as tightly as he could.

When the rocky shower ended moments later, he opened his eyes and looked up to find the seemingly elongated figure of Oren Hoover standing on the rim above him. Gabe looked down. The rocks lying so far below him seemed to be waiting, seemed to be beckoning to him. He looked up again when Hoover ground the heel of one of his boots into the back of his left hand.

Gabe cried out. He couldn't help himself. Much as he regretted the cry that pain had wrung from his lips as a sign of weakness, there was no way he could have prevented it. To strangle any other cry that he might emit, he clenched his teeth and pressed his forehead against the rocky wall of the canyon.

He endured the torture Hoover was inflicting on him. He continued to hold tightly to the outcropping as Hoover, without uttering a single word, continued to grind a boot heel into his hand. The pain was excruciating, but the Oglala warriors had taught him to endure pain.

Gabe heard movement above him. He opened his eyes and looked up. Hoover withdrew his boot heel. Then he seemed to shrink. Gabe realized that the man was hunkering down up there on the rim. He watched Hoover take one of his guns and grip it by the barrel instead of the butt. He knew what Hoover was about to do.

Hoover did it. He brought the butt of his revolver down on the back of Gabe's hand, almost smashing the bones in it.

Again, Gabe clenched his teeth to keep from crying out as he continued holding on. The gun butt came down again, even harder this time.

Hoover raised his gun butt. He was about to bring it down again on Gabe's hand when he stopped suddenly.

Gabe heard the sound of a shout.

At first, the words that had been shouted in a rough male voice didn't penetrate his consciousness. But when they were quickly repeated, they did.

"Get away from the edge, you bastard!"

Hoover's head swiveled around. He rose. He fired. His fire was returned. Gabe hunched his head down and pressed his face against the canyon wall as Hoover, arms and legs spread, soared out over the canyon's rim and began a swift descent, droplets of blood flying up into the air from the gaping wound in his chest as his body sailed relentlessly downward.

Gabe heard the explosive sound Hoover's body made as it struck the rocks below. He swallowed hard and then looked up to see the deputy he thought had been killed by Hoover back at the prison wagon staring down at him, a self-satisfied expression on his face.

"I thought—I thought," Gabe gasped, "you were dead."

"Wounded. Not dead. You got yourself in some fix, it sure does look like."

"Get me up out of here."

The deputy reached down and got a grip on Gabe's wrists with both of his hands. "Now you grab on to my wrists, and I'll pull you up."

When Gabe had done so, the deputy said, "Ready?" and, when Gabe nodded, he began to haul him upward.

It was slow going and once the deputy's hands, which were as sweaty as Gabe's, slipped. But the deputy persisted and slowly, little by little, Gabe's body rose and then, finally, he was lying prone on top of the rim. His breath came in short, shallow bursts as his chest heaved and his heart hammered.

He pushed himself up, got his knees under him, and rose. "I'm obliged to you," he said, and turned to find himself staring into the barrel of the deputy's gun.

"Let's go," the lawman said flatly.

Gabe suppressed both a sigh and any comments on jumping from frying pans into fires. He went to his dapple, climbed aboard it, and moved out on a snapped order from the deputy.

They had ridden no more than a half mile when the deputy said from behind Gabe, "I thought that fellow that freed you was a friend of yours."

"He wasn't."

"Who was he?"

"His name was Oren Hoover."

"How come he was trying to kill you when I tracked you both down?"

Gabe raised his right hand and felt the clotted blood on his neck where Hoover's bullet had grazed him. "Let's just say it was a personal matter."

"Grudge fight?"

"Just let it lie, will you, Deputy?"

"Well, all's well that ends well, as they say. He's dead and you're alive, and me, I've got my prisoner back. I've never lost a man yet, and I didn't intend to start that unhappy practice with you."

"I was sure Hoover had stopped your clock."

"For a second or two when he shot me, I thought he had, too. But when I realized I was still breathing, I decided I'd better play dead. I figured that would be my best chance for surviving with a wild dog like him around."

They rode on, not speaking anymore, until the prison wagon came into sight.

"Welcome back!" Rusty called out tauntingly as they approached it.

"We missed the pleasure of your pleasant company," Charlie added just as tauntingly.

Gabe dismounted without being told to do so and walked over to the wagon's barred door.

The deputy, key ring jingling in one hand, gun in the other, followed him on foot. The lawman unlocked the door of the wagon and, leaving the key ring dangling from the lock, motioned with his revolver for Gabe to enter the cage.

But Gabe had other ideas, and he chose that opportune moment to act on them. He stepped forward docilely, as if he were resigned to entering the prison. But instead of doing so, he swung a fist and knocked the gun from the deputy's hand. Before the shocked lawman could react, Gabe had ripped his own .44 from the man's waistband and used it to club the man into unconsciousness.

"Whoooeee!" Rusty crowed. "That was sure slick." He headed for the open door and freedom.

But Gabe picked up the unconscious deputy by the scruff of his neck and the seat of his pants and threw him into the wagon.

The man's limp body collided with the advancing Rusty, who was knocked backward into Charlie. All three men slammed into the wagon's bars behind them and went down in a pile of flailing limbs.

Gabe slammed the barred door shut and turned the deputy's key in the lock.

"Damn you!" Rusty shouted, his hands shaking the bars so violently that the entire wagon swayed. "Let me *out* of here!"

"I'm not about to do that," Gabe said placidly. "But somebody will. Sooner or later. All you got to do is hope it's sooner."

He held up the deputy's key ring. "I'll leave this right here on the ground, right next to his six-gun, and when somebody moseys along, why, you just ask him nice and polite to let you out and give you back your side arm."

As Rusty roared and cursed with rage, Gabe swung into the saddle and rode away.

He could still hear Rusty when he was a good half mile away from the prison wagon.

But at last the angry sound faded away, and Gabe traveled on through a peaceful land bright with sun and cheerful with birds singing. Off to his left, a quail rose out of the brush, winged along above the ground for a short distance, and then went to ground again. Watching its flight, Gabe's mouth began to water. Meat—a meal— on the wing. He considered riding in that direction, shooting the quail and cooking it. But he decided not to. He was not all that far away from the prison wagon yet and if, by any chance, the deputy managed to get free and came after him again, the sound of his shot would bring the lawman on the run for sure.

He would have to put more distance between himself and the law before he would be able to hunt with any sure sense of security. Meanwhile, there were bulbs and berries. They would have to do.

He kept his eyes peeled as he rode on, and in mid-afternoon he spotted some chickweed growing flat on the ground in a moist, shady spot. He drew rein and dismounted to gather some of the plant's green leaves, which he ate raw, remembering how the Oglala women used to boil the leaves of the chickweed plant and serve them mixed with buffalo grease.

When he had finished his bleak nooning, he stepped into the saddle and moved his dapple out, glancing over his shoulder as he did so.

There was no one on his back trail.

An hour later, he spotted riders coming toward him. It was too late for him to take cover; they would have seen him by now. He decided to play it cool.

As he came closer to the riders, he recognized them as Chickasaw Lighthorsemen. The policemen were riding in a double column the way cavalry troopers did. When they were almost upon him, Gabe waved to them. As nonchalantly as he could, he turned his horse and rode to the left, his trail making one arm of a widemouthed V with the trail the Chickasaw policemen were taking. No words had been exchanged.

The encounter stirred unpleasant thoughts in Gabe's mind. The Chickasaw Lighthorsemen, he thought, were nothing more than an armed force serving the white men who, when push came to shove, were the real rulers of the territories occupied by the Five Civilized Tribes, of which the Chickasaw were one. They had no jurisdiction over a white man who committed a crime against one of their own people, whether that crime was rape or murder or just simple theft. The jurisdiction in cases where a white person committed a crime against a Chickasaw citizen belonged to the federal court in Fort Smith, Arkansas, presided over by the notorious Judge Parker.

But, if a Chickasaw raped a white woman or murdered a white man, the Lighthorsemen could only apprehend the criminal; they could not prosecute him in their tribal courts. The Chickasaw in such a case also came under the jurisdiction of the Fort Smith court.

Didn't the Chickasaw see the discrimination involved in such a system? Gabe knew they did. But he also knew how fear and feelings of powerlessness could lead a people to compromise rather than be slaughtered. The great Oglala chief, Red Cloud, had finally compromised, given in.

Gabe drank the last of the warm water left in his canteen as he rode on, wondering where he was going, and ultimately deciding not to worry about choosing a specific destination. He would, he decided, drift for the time being.

With his thirst unappeased, his eyes roved the country-side in search of water. It was some time before he spotted some and then, when he arrived at the water hole, he discovered that it was covered with a green coating of algae across which water bugs skittered and scampered. Neither the bugs nor the algae bothered him. He got down from his horse and knelt at the edge of the water hole. He used his hands to clear a space on the water's surface and then he filled his canteen with some of the clear water that lay beneath the surface. He knew that such water was by far the safest to drink. A man might find a water hole with clear water in it and no trace of algae or insects upon its surface. But that water might well be alkaline. Where alage grew and insects lived—that water, he had long ago learned, was always sweet and safe to drink.

His growing hunger demanded that he shoot some game—if he could find any. He had spotted none by the time the sun had gone down. He was about ready to give up his desire for some meat when he spotted the tracks of an animal off to his right. He turned his dapple and rode over to them. The tracks' squarish pattern and their roughly triangular look told him that they had been left by a squirrel. A ground squirrel, not a tree squirrel. He looked around the area and then began to follow the tracks. Some distance away, he found the skeletal remains of an antelope and noted the teeth marks on the animal's horns, which confirmed his guess that he was trailing a ground squirrel.

The tracks ultimately led to a series of holes in the ground, some with piles of dirt in front of them, some with none. His horse stumbled as the soil gave way beneath it and its right front hoof sank six inches into the ground. Gabe drew his gun and halted his horse. An instant later, several squirrels, disturbed by the dapple's hoof intruding into their network of subterranean tunnels, scampered out of their burrows and ran for their lives.

One didn't make it. Gabe's second round brought it down, his first having missed its target. He rode to it, dismounted, and picked up his kill. Once in the saddle again, he rode on, until he came upon a grove of elms, into which he rode. There he built a small fire. As its smoke was dissipated by the leafy branches overhead, he skinned and gutted his kill and then spitted it and held it over the flames, turning it slowly.

Fat fell from the carcass into the fire where it sizzled and spat. When the meat was fully cooked, Gabe ate hungrily as darkness settled on the land. Soon, only a small pile of bones remained of the squirrel.

Gabe got his bedroll and spread it on the ground beneath the trees. He lay down and pulled his blanket around him as protection against the coolness of the night. He placed his gun belt and his hat next to his head. Above him the stars glittered in the sky and the moon, nearly full, sailed serenely.

He did not know how long he had been asleep when he was awakened by the faint sound of his horse softly nickering. He didn't move, didn't raise his head. But his eyes moved behind narrowed eyelids. He saw the dapple standing in the moonlight where he had picketed it. Its ears were erect as it stared into the darkness beyond the weak glow of the banked fire.

It nickered again, its ears flicking down to lie alongside its head and then up into the alert position again.

Gabe's hand snaked out from under his blanket and closed on the butt of his .44. He drew the gun to him. His ears strained to catch any sounds that were not a normal part of the night.

A twig snapped.

Gabe rolled to one side and came up behind the stout trunk of an old elm with his gun in both hands. His eyes gradually gained night vision despite the flickering of the fire. Its feeble light did nothing to keep him from seeing keenly in the darkness that was brightened somewhat in a few places by the light of the moon.

"Drop that gun!"

The words, spoken in a harsh male voice that Gabe recognized immediately, had come from behind him.

But he didn't drop his gun. Instead, he threw himself to the ground, rolled over, and came up again firing, as flashes of flame flew from the barrel of the gun in the hand of the deputy marshal Gabe had last seen when he had locked him in his own prison wagon.

CHAPTER SIX

Bright flashes of gunfire continued to illuminate the night.

From behind the cover of the elm tree's trunk, Gabe took time out from the deadly gun battle with the deputy to reload. Quickly he thumbed cartridges out of his gun belt and filled the empty chambers of his revolver's cylinder. He guessed that the deputy might be doing the same since the night was now silent.

But the gunfire erupted again.

Gabe was surprised to find that it was coming from an entirely different direction than it had been previously. Now it was coming from the northeast. Before it had been coming at him from the south. Had the deputy shifted position? That made no sense to Gabe. If he had, he had no better chance of drilling his target from his new position than he had had from his old.

Gabe decided to find out exactly where the man was. "How'd you get out of your cage, lawdog?" he called out.

For a moment he received no reply. Then the deputy bellowed, "The country's full of Good Samaritans, that's how. A drifter came by and let me out. But the greedy bastard wouldn't do it until I'd forked over ten dollars."

"I'm surprised you found me, it being about as dark as the pit out tonight," Gabe called out when he realized that the deputy was still in the same spot. His eyes shifted to the left and right, but he saw no sign of anyone else in the immediate vicinity.

"In my business," the deputy yelled, "one thing a man's got to be is a good tracker. And I can, if I do say so myself, track bees through a blizzard."

Who had fired the shots that had come from the northeast? Gabe asked himself. Well, he thought, there was one way to find out. Maybe he could make whoever had fired them show himself. He fired in that direction— a single shot.

It brought an answering volley that flew harmlessly past his position, although two of the shots slammed into the trunk of the elm, sending slivers of wood flying into the air.

"Who's siding you to the northeast, lawdog?" Gabe called out.

"Me," a male voice called out.

"Me, too," another voice chimed in. The second voice had come from the west.

Gabe recognized both voices. The one from the northeast belonged to the prisoner named Rusty and the other one to his friend, Charlie.

"It appears that Good Samaritan you mentioned," Gabe

called to the deputy, "let more than just you out of that prison wagon."

"I let those two bad boys out myself," the deputy responded.

Rusty giggled and then shouted, "We've been deputized. Now we're lawmen, too."

Well, I'll be damned, Gabe thought. He fired first at the deputy's position, then at Rusty's, then at Charlie's. His last shot brought a yelp of pain from his target. Bull's-eye. He fired in that direction again.

Charlie screamed. He stood up, so that he was just barely visible to Gabe in the thin moonlight. He stood almost motionless for a moment, and then he swayed and fell to the ground.

"You killed him!" Rusty screeched. "You killed my friend!"

Gabe hugged the tree trunk as Rusty fired off a fast volley of shots in his direction. One down, two to go, he thought, and fired at the deputy, whose hat brim now jutted out from one side of the boulders was hidden behind.

His shot struck stone instead of flesh. He reloaded. Waited.

Both men fired at him. Both missed him. He continued waiting, hoping that one of them would run out of patience and make a move that would make him an easier target. When neither man did, when both men continued firing, pausing only long enough to reload their weapons, he decided it was up to him to make a move.

He turned around and crawled along the ground, heading away from the elm tree. He shoved underbrush out of his way as it clawed at his face, and then, when he was sure he was out of range of both the deputy's and Rusty's guns, he straightened up and went loping silently through the night. He moved with a fluid grace and used all the skills he had learned as a boy among the Oglala not to betray his position. He circled around, and ten minutes later, as the moon rode into a cove of clouds, he was behind the deputy's position and a little bit above it.

He opened his eyes wide and scanned the area directly below and in front of him.

There!

Off to the left was the deputy. The man was crouching down low, occasionally risking a peek over the top of the boulders, and also occasionally squeezing off a shot at the elm tree where he obviously assumed Gabe still remained.

"Cover me!" the man suddenly bellowed to Rusty. Then he was up and charging forward toward the elm tree.

Rusty simultaneously fired several shots at the elm. They all plowed into the tree's trunk.

Gabe leveled his gun and took aim at the running deputy. But then he slowly lowered it. Something made it impossible for him to shoot the man in the back. When the deputy, his six-gun blazing, rounded the elm and silence fell again, Gabe retraced his steps, heading back toward the position he had so recently left.

He had almost reached it when he heard a shot and a shout. Both had come from some distance away from his own present position. Who had fired and who had shouted?

"I got him!" Rusty yelled. "By God in His great Heaven, I got the bastard!"

So, Gabe thought, it was Rusty who had fired the shot. Then it must have been the deputy who had shouted. But why?

"You didn't," the deputy called out, his voice rising and falling in an unnatural pattern. "You got *me*!"

Gabe raced on until he was able to see the deputy lying on the ground midway between the elm tree and his former position. Apparently the man had decided, when he reached the elm and didn't find Gabe behind it, to return to his original position. And Rusty, in the darkness, had shot him down, thinking he was shooting at Gabe.

"Deputy?" Rusty's tentatively spoken word pierced the night.

The deputy's reply was an almost inaudible gurgle followed by an ominous silence.

"Oh, Jesus bleeding Christ, I killed him!" Rusty cried.

Gabe fired at the spot where the sound had come from.

"Don't!" Rusty screamed. "Don't shoot me! I give up! Do you hear me? I've had enough. I don't want to die, damn it! I'm leaving. I don't want no more part of this. All I ever wanted was my freedom. Well, I've got it, and I ain't going to do no more shooting. *You hear me?*"

Rusty's last few words were spoken frantically.

"I hear you," Gabe answered. "But I don't hear you leaving."

"I'm throwing down the gun the deputy gave me. I'm going. Good-bye!"

Gabe listened to the sound of Rusty thrashing his way through the underbrush. He held his gun steady as the sounds gradually grew fainter and finally faded altogether.

Gabe didn't move for several more minutes. He continued listening until he was finally satisfied that Rusty had made good on his promise to vamoose. Then he walked over to where the deputy lay on the ground. He hunkered down and placed two fingers on the side of the man's neck. No pulse. He did the same for Charlie with the same result.

Rising, he holstered his .44 and made his way over to where he had left his dapple. He pulled the picket pin and spent some time rubbing the horse down with grass before getting it ready to ride.

But before he could ride out, he became aware of a man standing immobile some distance away, silently watching him.

His hand dropped to the butt of his gun.

The man's eyes widened, and he quickly threw up his hands. "Don't shoot," he said.

"What are you doing here?" Gabe asked him.

"Just passing through. Heard the shooting and came to see what was going on."

Gabe studied the man. He was tall and solidly built, probably on the short side of fifty. His eyes were black and so was the stubble covering his plump cheeks and jutting jaw. He wore clothes that had seen better days and too many trails. He wore no gun.

Gabe stepped into the saddle. Before he could move his dapple out, the man stepped forward and said, "I left my horse back there among the trees. Would you mind if I rode along with you for a spell?"

Gabe hesitated. He didn't want company. But he also

didn't want to be surly. "Suit yourself," he said finally and waited as the man disappeared among the trees and then reappeared in a few minutes aboard a gray gelding.

"I'll feel safe in your company, sir," the man said as he joined Gabe and they moved out, "since the wicked are abroad in the land. As the Good Book says: 'The wicked are estranged from the womb; they go astray as soon as they be born, speaking lies. Their poison is like the poison of a serpent.' Psalm fifty-eight, verses three and four."

"How do you know I'm not the wicked one, not those two dead men or the one that ran off?"

The man's jaw dropped. He gave Gabe a sidelong glance. "I thought—"

"Out here in the West it's not a good idea to get your exercise jumping to conclusions. It could buy you a peck of trouble."

The man hesitated a moment and then said, "Maybe I ought to change the subject. Maybe we could talk about—oh, I don't know. The weather?"

Gabe didn't respond.

"It's been mild of late," his companion commented. "But have you seen the caterpillars? They've got heavy coats. That's a sure sign that the winter's going to be bad. Cold. Snowy. I hate the winter. It digs down deep into my bones, and I can't seem to get warm from early October until well on into April."

Still Gabe said nothing.

His companion talked on about everything and nothing, his voice a dull drone.

Magpie, Gabe thought. He chatters like one. He tried

to think of other things. But the other things that came unbidden into his mind were also unwanted. Images of death—the corpses that littered the trail behind him. Wes Harrison, Archie Hoover, Oren Hoover, the deputy, and his prisoner, Charlie.

The man at his side was still talking—about the lay of the land and about the desperadoes that infested that land—when the sun began to rise. Within the hour, it was blazing. Gabe drank from his canteen and then offered it to his companion, who emptied it.

"Hot for this time of year," the man remarked. "Maybe those caterpillars I mentioned a while back have got things wrong. Maybe it won't be such a bad winter after all. Which would be good news for my aging bones to hear, I can tell you."

Gabe watched the sky. After a while, he saw what he had hoped to see—a flock of birds. He turned his horse and headed in the direction the birds were taking.

"Where are you going?" the man next to him asked anxiously. "Is something amiss?"

"Water," Gabe said. "Over that way. See there—where those birds are dropping down?"

"Well, I'll be dogged," the man said. "You certainly know a lot about the wilderness."

"I know that birds go to water in the morning and evening."

"I knew I had done well to join forces with you. I'm awfully thirsty, and that's a fact."

The two men sent the birds flapping into the sky as they arrived at the water hole.

Gabe slid out of the saddle and led his horse to the water. As the dapple stepped hock-deep into the water and lowered its head to drink, Gabe knelt and scooped water up in his hands. He tasted it and, finding it sweet, drank. He was filling his canteen when he saw a shadow fall over the water's surface directly in front of him.

He saw the shadow raise both arms above its head. . . .

He spun around, going for his gun. . . .

But he was too late.

The rock in the hands of the man who had been riding with him crashed down upon the top of his head, crushing his hat and almost cracking his skull.

He lost consciousness immediately.

When Gabe awoke, he found he could not move. He raised his head and saw that he was spread-eagled on the ground. His wrists and ankles were tied with strips of rawhide to wooden stakes pounded into the hardpan. There was also a broad strip of rawhide tied around his forehead. And one encircling his chest.

From where he lay on his back on the ground, he could see his hat, cartridge belt, and .44 lying nearby. Farther away were his dapple and the gray gelding his companion on the trail had been riding.

" 'If anyone slays with the sword, with the sword must he be slain.' "

Gabe strained his neck and saw the man he had been riding with, the man who had attacked him, standing just beyond his head. "Revelations, chapter thirteen, verse ten, Mr. Conrad."

"You know me."

"I know you. Not well. But well enough. I know that you killed my son, Archie. I found his grave marker."

"You're—"

"Caleb Hoover's my name. I sent my other son to track you. His name is Oren, but I gather he failed to find you."

"Oh, he found me all right."

Hoover walked around to take up a position in front of Gabe. "Oren found you?"

"He did. He's dead."

"You also killed Oren?" Hoover shrieked, his face reddening.

Gabe told him what had happened to Oren. When he had finished, he watched Hoover bow his head and move his lips, apparently in prayer. When the man raised his head again, Gabe asked, "How'd you find me?"

"I sent Oren after you. But I couldn't sit and wait for him to return. I set out after him. I made inquiries. People who had seen him directed me to him. But then I lost his trail. I wandered about, asking if anyone had seen you—or Oren. It was not until I ran into a column of Chickasaw Lighthorsemen and asked if they had seen you that I was put once again on your trail. Then I heard shooting and arrived in time to witness the battle between you and those three men back there."

"You mean to take vengeance on me."

"Justice, Mr. Conrad, not vengeance. When the Lord spoke of Abraham in the book of Genesis, He said, in part, 'For I know him, that he will command his children and his household after him, and they shall keep the way of the Lord, to do justice and judgment.' "

"You may call it justice if that suits you; I call it vengeance."

"As you wish, Mr. Conrad. But I, like Abraham of old, taught my sons the ways of justice and judgment.

Now that they are gone—because of you—I am the lone instrument of such justice and judgment remaining."

"What are you going to do to me?"

"I'm going to watch you die. Those rawhide bands— I soaked them in water before I tied them around your head and chest. The sun's hot. They'll start drying out soon. And when they do, well, they're going to tighten up, bit by little bit, and you're going to be hurting real bad before long."

Gabe was aware that the bands had tightened noticeably since he had regained consciousness.

"Then I've also got another little treat in store for you. Your dying is going to be slow, Mr. Conrad. It's going to be real bad. I'm going to take my knife, and I'm going to start making cuts on your body. Like this."

Hoover took a knife from a sheath on his belt and reached out with it.

Gabe stared at the blade that was inches above his throat as the sun glinted on it. He bit his lower lip to keep from crying out when Hoover made a cut in the skin of his neck just below his Adam's apple.

The blade descended again. This time Hoover cut Gabe's left wrist.

He could feel the blood begin to seep from both wounds.

"Yes, sir, Mr. Conrad," Hoover said gleefully, "you're going to be a long time dying. While you are, I want you to concentrate your mind on why all this is happening to you. I want you to think about how you killed my two sons. Yes, Mr. Conrad, as the Bible says—in Ezekiel, I believe—'The soul that sinneth, it shall die.' "

Hoover sat down cross-legged on the ground. He stared

fixedly at Gabe, his eyes never wavering, hardly even seeming to blink.

But Gabe turned his attention from his tormentor to his own desperate predicament. His head was beginning to ache and his chest was starting to constrict painfully as the rawhide bands continued to shrink. He strained against the rawhide thongs that were tied to his wrists and ankles. They did not give. He twisted his hands and feet but to no avail. Then he tried to pull the stakes the thongs were tied to out of the ground. Again, to no avail.

He forced himself to relax. He tried not to think about the hot sun that was blazing down upon him where he lay so helplessly. Sweat rolled down his face. It began to dampen his clothes.

"Archie was a good boy," Hoover intoned as he continued to watch his prisoner. "Always ready to lend his father a hand. Same with Oren. Both of them were good boys. A father couldn't want for better sons. They were a comfort to me. Like balm of Gilead. But you, Mr. Conrad, you saw fit to take them from me. Not one of them, but both. So surely you can understand why I am sorely vexed with you."

Gabe closed his eyes, trying to squeeze from them the stinging sweat that had run into them. His head seemed about to burst. The rawhide band that encircled it continued to squeeze it. There was not a moment of relief. The pressure increased minute by agonizing minute. He felt a scream welling up in his throat. But he realized he did not have the breath with which to utter it as his chest was also constricted in the grip of the leather band surrounding it.

"Make him suffer, o Lord," Hoover prayed, his hands clasped together in front of him. "Scourge him, o Lord, that he may come to see and understand the error of his ways and repent."

Gabe tried to lick his parched lips, but could not gather enough saliva to do so because the sun was squeezing every bit of water from his pores as it burned relentlessly down upon him. A drumming began in his skull. It pulsed there, growing louder by the minute. He was being forced to take shallow breaths now because he could no longer expand his lungs normally as the rawhide encircling his torso grew even tighter as the sun sucked more and more of the moisture from it.

The sky above him lurched. It began to spin.

I'm passing out, he thought with a sense of rising panic. If I do, I might never wake up again. He struggled again in an attempt to free his hands and feet. Did one of the thongs binding his right wrist give a little? Or did he only imagine it did? He pulled on it again as hard as he could, straining with all his might. It *did* give! Not much. But a little. Hope blazed in him.

He cried out in pain as Hoover made another cut in his flesh—this time in his left forearm. And still another one in his right forearm.

"Let the fluids that sustain life leave him, o just and righteous Lord," Hoover cried wildly. "Let him sweat. Let him bleed. Let him *die*!"

Gabe, despite the pain that was squeezing his skull as the rawhide dried and tightened around it, worked hard at freeing his right wrist. He twisted it as hard as he could in one direction and then twisted it just as hard in the opposite direction. The stake remained in place. But not firmly in place.

Beside him, Hoover, his head tilted back at a sharp angle, his gaze cast heavenward and his hands clasped tightly in front of his chest, continued his terrible prayers.

"Let him not die too soon, o mighty Lord. Let him, instead, live to suffer as he has made me suffer because of the loss of my two fine sons. Let a hundred cuts in his flesh be not too many. Let a thousand be not enough."

Gabe tugged as hard as he could, and the stake nearly popped out of the ground. But at that instant Hoover lowered his head and looked down on him with malevolence alive in his bitter black eyes.

Gabe's hand stilled. He lay there, not moving a muscle, feeling the blood seep from the knife cuts Hoover had made in his body. Feeling, too, the drumming in his skull caused by the shrinking rawhide. His breath was coming now in shallow gasps, like those that might have come from a broken bellows.

Hoover raised the knife in his hand. He ran his left index finger along the edge of its sharp blade. "When I am through with you, Mr. Conrad, you will rue the day you were born. You will be crying out for mercy, but there will be no mercy for you. None."

Hoover, his black eyes bright and filled with hate, lowered the knife in his hands toward his captive's face.

Gabe waited until the deadly blade was only inches away from his face before he acted. Then he jerked the stake which had held his right wrist nearly immobile out of the ground. He seized Hoover's wrist, stopping the knife's descent.

"No!" Hoover shrieked, his face flushing.

"Yes," Gabe hissed, as he slammed Hoover's hand into the ground and the knife fell from it. "*Yes!*"

Releasing his hold on Hoover's wrist, he picked up the knife. Before Hoover knew what was happening, Gabe had sliced through the rawhide that bound his left wrist. He sat up and shoved Hoover, the palm of his left hand slamming into the man's chest to send him toppling over backward. Then he deftly sliced through the thongs that bound his ankles.

As Hoover got up on his hands and knees, Gabe leapt to his feet and kicked out. His boot caught Hoover under the chin and sent him flying backward, to lie moaning and retching on the ground some distance away.

Gabe severed the length of rawhide that bound his chest and then did the same for the leather encircling his skull. Panting, he stood, with Hoover's knife still in his hand, staring down at his tormentor.

"What—what are you going to do?" Hoover managed to stammer as he returned Gabe's stony stare.

"I ought to kill you. I ought to kill you slow like you were bound and determined to do to me. In fact, I think I will."

As Gabe lunged for Hoover, meaning to terrorize but not really kill him, Hoover let out a wild cry of alarm and rolled to one side. He came up then, his right hand groping frantically inside his coat. When that hand emerged a split second later, it had a gun in it. He fired at Gabe with the .45 he had taken from his hidden shoulder holster.

The round, because of Hoover's unsteady stance, went wild.

Before Hoover could fire a second time, Gabe threw

the knife. It flew end over end through the air and struck Hoover in the left shoulder. It bit into the man's flesh and stayed there.

The gun fell from Hoover's hand as he stared in disbelief at his own knife protruding from his flesh. Then he looked back at Gabe. When he saw that Gabe had turned and retrieved his .44 from where it lay not far from where he had been staked out, Hoover let out a scream of fear and rage.

He ripped the knife from his shoulder and went after Gabe.

"Back off, or I'll drill you!" Gabe warned him.

Hoover skidded to an abrupt halt. He stood there, his body rigid, his eyes on the gun in Gabe's hand, and then, looking up, he did what Gabe had just done. He threw the knife.

Gabe swiftly sidestepped the oncoming blade.

As it fell harmlessly to the ground, Hoover turned and fled toward his horse.

Gabe took aim at the man and fired, a shot not meant to kill but to spur Hoover on in his frantic flight. The ploy worked. Hoover scrambled clumsily into the saddle and galloped away.

"If you come back, old man," Gabe yelled after him, "I won't miss next time. I'll shoot to kill, and you'll die just like your two murderous sons did."

Gabe tossed the knife away from him. Then he went to where his hat lay on the ground. He picked it up, slapped it against his thigh to rid it of dust, and clapped it on his head. He retrieved his gun belt and strapped it on, adjusting it so that it rode at a comfortable level on his lean hips.

He drew his own knife and cut away the remnants of the rawhide thongs from his wrists and ankles. Then he went to his dapple and stepped into the saddle.

That afternoon he crossed the border into Choctaw Nation and soon after that he rode into Springtown, a stop on the Missouri, Kansas, and Texas Railroad. He stopped at the first restaurant he came to and ordered a huge meal: steak, dumplings, boiled rice, and caramel-glazed carrots. He ate like a man famished, and it was not until he had forked the last of the food into his mouth and sopped up the steak's juices with a thick piece of brown bread that his hunger was at last appeased.

He beckoned to the waiter.

Now, what's wrong with that fella? Gabe wondered. He looks like he's about to bolt. Do I look like that much of a desperado after my long time on the trail? Or is he just naturally leery of strangers? If he is, he oughtn't to be in the restaurant business.

He beckoned again, and this time the waiter sidled up to his table. "How much do I owe you?" he asked the man.

"That'll be four bits for the food and ten cents extra for the coffee."

Gabe paid his bill.

I need a shave and a haircut, he thought. Something to make me look presentable so I won't scare the wits out of waiters and stray dogs.

Once outside the restaurant, he asked a man passing by which of the two hotels facing each other on opposite sides of the street was the better one.

"Neither one's much to write home about," the man

replied. "They're both lousy."

Gabe shrugged and headed for the one on the opposite side of the street. As he did so, he noticed that people on the street—some of them, at any rate—seemed to be giving him uneasy looks and sidelong glances. Not one of them had looked directly into his eyes. He wondered if it was because they were mostly Choctaw and he was a white man. But that couldn't account for their odd behavior. The Nations were full of white men and a few white women.

"Hey, you!" a young man of about nineteen or twenty straight ahead of him called out. "Gabe Conrad!"

Gabe halted, stunned by the fact that a man he didn't know, one he had never seen before in his life as far as he could recall, had just addressed him by name.

The man who had called his name drew a gun and took aim at Gabe. Gabe's gun quickly cleared leather. He leveled it at the man who had been about to shoot him.

"You might kill me," Gabe called out, "but be warned. I'll take you down with me."

The young man's gun hand began to tremble.

"What's this all about?" Gabe asked him.

At first, the man didn't answer. When he did answer moments later, his answer took the form of a thumb jerked over his shoulder. Then he fled, his gun still in his hand.

What, Gabe wondered, had the man meant by his gesture? He walked on and stopped where the man had been standing when he had drawn his gun.

At first, he didn't notice it. But then, after carefully scanning the area in an effort to understand what had just happened, Gabe's eyes fell on the dodger nailed to a post helping to support the overhang in front of a tin shop. He walked over to it and read what was printed on it:

WANTED DEAD OR ALIVE—GABE CONRAD
Conrad is wanted for the cold-blooded murder of one Jerry Rutledge in Tishomingo, Chickasaw Nation, and for escaping from the custody of a United States Deputy Marshal. He is armed and deemed exceedingly dangerous. Conrad is believed to be in the Nations. A reward of one thousand dollars is being offered by the federal government to any individual who can apprehend him and turn him over—dead or alive—to the duly constituted authorities.

The dodger concluded with a detailed and precise physical description of Gabe and of the clothes he had been wearing when last seen.

No wonder the waiter in the restaurant seemed scared of me, Gabe thought. He must have recognized me from this wanted poster.

CHAPTER SEVEN

"It's him!" someone shouted.

Gabe turned and saw the young man who had drawn on him pointing at him as he yelled again to several men standing on the boardwalk, "It's Gabe Conrad! He's wanted. Dead or alive!"

As the young man ducked down behind a water trough and his gun rose above it, Gabe took cover behind a crate sitting under the overhang in front of the tin shop. His gun, which was still in his hand, swiveled around in the direction of the water trough.

For a moment, no one fired. Then several shots rang out. They came from several guns belonging to men who had been alerted by the young man to Gabe's presence on the main street of Springtown.

All of the shots went past Gabe, but one came dangerously close to him as it buried itself in the wood of the crate. He returned the fire, not aiming to kill, but hoping to run off the men who were out to collect the price on his head. His shots momentarily deterred them, apparently, since there was no more shooting.

Then the young man yelled from behind the water trough, "We can split the bounty money amongst ourselves. What do you boys say to that proposition?"

"It's okay by me," one of the men yelled back.

"Henry Blount's in on the deal," the young man called out. "What about you, Rossiter?"

"I'm in," the man named Rossiter replied and punctuated his reply by squeezing off a shot, which whined past Gabe, still hunkered down behind the crate.

"Anybody else ready, willing, and able to throw in with us to bring Conrad down?" the young man yelled.

"Count me in," a man called out from an alley across the street.

"Anybody else?" the young man shouted. When no one else answered him, he continued, "That makes four of us. Bill Soames in the alley, Henry Blount in the doorway of the hotel, Rossiter down by the livery, and me right here. Let's rush him, boys, what do you say?"

"Maybe we can pick him off from where we are," Rossiter responded. "We move out into the open, and he can gun us down without no trouble a'tall."

"But there's four of us against his one," Blount countered. "I say we rush him. He can't kill all of us."

"But I don't fancy being the one he might kill," Rossiter complained.

More rounds were fired then from four different locations. None came from Gabe's position.

For several minutes there was silence. All the bystanders had fled the boardwalks lining both sides of the street. The four would-be bounty hunters were not visible. Neither was Gabe.

"This ain't getting us nowhere," Blount yelled. "I say

we rush him. I'm all for pocketing a share of that bounty money."

"Me, too," the young man cried. "Split four ways, it'll come to over two hundred dollars apiece. And if one of us should get killed, it'll come to over *three* hundred!"

"You're so all-fired money-hungry," Rossiter yelled, "go ahead and act the fool. I'm not moving out into the open against no gunslick like that Conrad fella. I aim to stay in one piece awhile longer."

"How about the rest of you?" the young man shouted. "Blount? Soames?"

"You call it, Cully," Soames yelled back. "We'll be right behind you."

There was a moment of silence, and then Cully yelled, "*Now!*"

He sprang up from behind the water trough, gun blazing, and went racing toward the tin shop. Behind him came Henry Blount, who had emerged from the hotel's doorway, and Soames, who ran out of the alley across the street.

The sound of gunfire was as deafening as the stench of gun smoke was overpowering.

"Where the hell is he?" Soames asked when the three men had converged on the crate under the tin shop's overhang and found no one behind it.

"He's given us the slip," Cully lamented, looking around.

"We'd best take cover," Henry Blount suggested nervously. "There's no telling where he might be."

"There he is!" Cully yelped and pointed to where Gabe was running from one side of the street to the other in the distance. He was moving fast from the side on which the tin shop was located to the side where the restaurant in which he had eaten was located.

While the four men had been busy arguing their strategy, Gabe had slipped unnoticed out from behind the crate and into the tin shop. Ordering the customers and tinsmith he found inside to remain calm and quiet, he loped through the shop and out its back door. He turned right and ran down the line of stores' back doors until he was sure he was out of range of any revolvers that might be fired at him from the vicinity of the tin shop. Holstering his .44, he turned right again and headed for the main street. Before crossing it, he peered around the corner of the last store in the line and saw three of the bounty hunters standing under the tin shop's overhang.

He sprinted across the street and swore when he heard Cully shout and realized he had been spotted. He had hoped to make it back to his dapple at the hitch rail in front of the restaurant without being seen.

He glanced at the three men who were racing down the street in his direction and then ducked behind the wall of a drugstore that was, he estimated, about nine doors away from the restaurant. He ran until he was behind the building and then started to sprint toward the restaurant in the distance.

He had not gone more than twenty paces when a man leapt out from between two of the buildings ahead of him and leveled a carbine at him. As the man sighted and began to squeeze the trigger, Gabe threw himself against the wall of a store and flattened himself there.

The shot the man fired *pinged* past him.

He left the wall and ran toward his assailant. Halfway to the man, he sprang upward and seized the overhang at the rear of one of the stores with both hands. He hauled himself up and, once on top of the tar paper roof, he ran, arms spread to help maintain his balance, to the end of the overhang. There he leapt to another overhang jutting out from the next shop in line. Then he leapt down from it onto the man with the carbine.

They both hit the ground. Gabe came up moments later with the carbine he had wrested from the man in his hands. He slammed it against the wall of a store and, when it splintered, he dropped it and threw a roundhouse right that sent the gun's owner spinning into unconsciousness.

Gabe ran on. He was almost to his destination— the restaurant—when someone yelled from behind him. "Shoot him, Soames!"

He glanced over his shoulder and saw Cully and Soames standing some distance behind him. Soames was gripping a six-gun in both hands and taking aim.

Gabe drew his .44 and fired a well-aimed round that knocked the revolver out of Soames's hand and sent him, yelping with fright, and Cully, face ashen, diving for cover into the alley from which they had emerged.

If this keeps up, Gabe thought, as he ran on toward the restaurant, I'll have more corpses to my credit than I want to count. These bounty hunters seem bound and determined to make me shoot them down dead. I'll turn out to have a reputation worse than Wes Hardin or Doc Holliday.

He reached the rear of the restaurant and halted. He peered cautiously around the corner of the building next door. No one in sight. He loped down the alley. When he reached the main street, he stopped and surveyed the street. There was no one on it. A man appeared in the window of the dry goods store across the street, but when he saw Gabe, he withdrew.

Gabe stepped out of the alley, freed his dapple from the hitch rail in front of the restaurant, and stepped into the saddle.

As he did so, Cully and Soames emerged from the alley where they had taken cover. Both men fired at him. He ducked down low and went galloping down the street away from the two men, one of whom—he didn't see which—let out a wail of frustration followed by a string of vivid curses.

As he rode out of town, Gabe glanced over his shoulder. At first, he thought no one was coming after him. But minutes later, he heard the sound of horse's hooves pounding the ground behind him.

This time it was his turn to curse. He rode on, turning and firing at his pursuers, which included the apparently recovered man he had decked behind the shops who, he supposed, was Blount.

All three fired a volley of shots at him which thundered in the air, but none of them were marksmen and their wildly fired and poorly aimed rounds did Gabe no damage.

He lashed the withers of his dapple with his reins, and the horse responded gamely with a renewed burst of speed that took it and Gabe around a bend and up a rise. He doubled back when he reached the top of the rise. He doubled back when he reached the top of the rise and rode along the ridge above the trail he had been following, which was not far below him. He kept well back from the rim in order not to be seen. When he came to a spot where some frost-cracked boulders lay, he drew rein sharply. He leapt to the ground while the dapple was still moving and peered over the rim.

His three pursuers were still coming hell-bent for election, he saw. Not one of them had the good sense to slow down as they approached the bend in case he might be waiting for them there, ready to blow them all, one right after the other, into eternity. As bounty hunters and gunslicks all three would make good ribbon clerks.

Gabe put a shoulder against one of the broken boulders and shoved. The boulder didn't move. He shoved harder and this time the boulder did move. He kept shoving, beginning to pant with the effort he was making, and managed to maneuver the boulder up to the edge of the drop. Without hesitation, he pushed it over and watched it bounce loudly down the steep slope. The three riders below were looking up at it with awe in their eyes.

That awe turned to terror as the boulder came closer and closer to them. Cully tried to outrun it. Soames made the stupid mistake of drawing rein, as if that would somehow save him from the half ton of rock that was bounding so swiftly down toward him. The third man lost control of his horse, which bolted at the sight and sound of the oncoming boulder, and he fell to the ground in front of Cully's horse, which trampled him before galloping on.

The boulder struck Soames broadside. The man gave an abortive scream as he was knocked from his horse which, in turn, was knocked down and carried along the ground by the boulder's momentum.

Cully looked up and saw Gabe on the ridge. "Damn your eyes!" he screamed and fired.

Gabe merely leaned back, and the round went screaming by him. He leaned forward and, drawing his gun, shot Cully's horse in the head. The animal dropped like a stone, catching Cully's right leg beneath its lifeless bulk.

Gabe surveyed the area directly below him. His three pursuers no longer represented a threat to him, he decided. Soames appeared to be dead.

Blount was calling weakly for help as he gripped his gut with both hands and blood dripped from his lips. Cully remained pinned beneath his dead horse.

Gabe left the rim and stepped back into the saddle. He rode out, leaving the three men—what was left of them—behind him.

That's three bounty hunters out of commission, he thought with grim satisfaction as he traveled on. But how many more have seen that dodger on me? How many are riding my back trail right this minute? How many am I liable to run into up ahead before I've gone very far?

The answers that came to him were unsettling. If the dodger was posted in Choctaw Nation, when the crime for which he was wanted had occurred in Chickasaw Nation, Gabe was almost positive that the dodger would also be posted in the other three nations, not to mention Texas and other jurisdictions.

There was not likely to be, for the time being at any rate, a safe place where he could go to ground. Certainly not in the cities. He could live alone off the land for a long time; his Oglala brothers had taught him how to do that.

He thought of Jerry Rutledge and the way the man had

thrown down on him in Tishomingo. He could see Pearl Rutledge's face in his mind's eye. He wished she were here now. If she were, he would wring her neck as he would a chicken's.

He made up his mind. He would go to Tishomingo, and he would find Pearl, and when he did he would . . .

Gabe kept trying—and failing—to make himself comfortable on the stiff seat he occupied in a coach of the Missouri, Kansas, and Texas Railroad. He had flagged the train down due south of Springtown and, despite the grumbling of the conductor about passengers "who can't board at a depot in town like they're supposed to do," he managed to get his dapple into one of the empty slatted stock cars before climbing aboard the train himself.

He watched the scenery sail by outside the grimy window on his right and thought of what awaited him when he arrived in Tishomingo. Pearl Rutledge awaited him. But this time there would be no sweet dalliance between them as there had been the last time they had met. This time it would be strictly business. He couldn't help giving a sigh of regret; Pearl had been a prize package, no two ways about that.

Three fellow travelers across the aisle from him bought a bar of soap, a towel, and a tin dish, which they proceeded to take turns using in an attempt to rid themselves, as much as possible, of the grime that was an inescapable fact of life aboard a train. Other passengers bought candy, cigars, and other sundries.

Soon the conductor barged into the swaying coach and called out, "Next stop, Atoka. Atoka is the next stop, ladies and gentlemen."

Later, as the train pulled into the depot at Atoka amid
a shower of sparks from its screeching wheels on the iron
tracks as the brakes were applied, Gabe leapt down onto
the platform and went to the stock car. He slid back the
door of the car and pulled out the wooden ramp. He set
it in place and then led his horse out of the car. He tossed
the ramp back inside the car, closed the door, and left his
horse hitched to the ground while he went to buy a ticket
on the line to Boggy Depot.

"Here you are, sir," the ticket clerk said as he handed
over the ticket. "The train's not due until one-fourteen
this afternoon."

Gabe leaned down and peered through the ticket window at the clock inside the office. It was only twenty
minutes after ten.

"How long's it take to get from here to Boggy Depot?"
he asked the ticket clerk.

"Little over an hour if the train doesn't go off the
track, as it is wont to do at times."

A grim-faced Gabe sat down on a wooden bench on
the platform to wait.

The train arrived on time and Gabe, after placing his
horse in one of its freight cars, boarded it. An hour or
so later they reached Boggy Depot—without mishap.

He walked his horse to the livery near the station and
paid the livery man there to feed and water the animal.
"Rub him down good while you're at it," he instructed
the man. "I'll be back for him in an hour."

He made his way to a restaurant where he ate a hearty
meal and then to a barbershop where he paid two bits for
a bath and the same amount for a shave and a haircut. No

use looking like some saddle tramp when he eventually met again with Pearl Rutledge.

He rode into Tishomingo the following morning. The sun was out of sight behind a dark gray sky that threatened an early and unseasonable snow. He made his way to the Central Hotel, where he had stayed the last time he was in town. Leaving his horse hitched outside the building, he entered the lobby and spoke to the desk clerk.

"You know a Mrs. Pearl Rutledge." It was a statement, not a question.

"Yes, I do," the man responded.

"I want to talk to her. Where does she live?"

"I'm not at liberty to give out that information. Mrs. Rutledge wouldn't want me to."

Gabe leaned over the desk. He moved the guest book aside. And the inkwell. Then he reached out and seized the desk clerk by the shirt and dragged him halfway across the desk toward him.

"What—stop—"

"Shut your mouth, mister!" Gabe muttered in the man's face. "Now, I'm going to ask you one more time and one more time only where Mrs. Rutledge lives. If you're still disinclined to answer, I'm going to bust your skull wide open and let your brains, if you've got any, fall out on the floor."

"Let me go! Put me down!"

"Not until you tell me what I need to know."

The desk clerk gave him Pearl's address and then, in response to his query, told him how to find her house. Gabe let him go and strode out of the hotel, thinking,

Pearl, honey, here I come, ready or not.

Following the directions he had gotten from the desk clerk, he soon found the Rutledge residence. It was a white frame house with black shutters on its windows, surrounded by a white picket fence. Gabe went through the gate in the fence and up the walk to the house. He climbed up onto the porch and knocked on the front door.

It was opened a moment later by Pearl Rutledge, who had a welcoming smile on her face—until she saw who was standing outside. Her smile died as she gave a shocked cry and tried to slam the door shut. But Gabe got his foot between it and the jamb and then thrust it wide open. Shoving the mewling Pearl aside, he strode into the house and slammed the door behind him.

"Don't hurt me!" Pearl whimpered, one hand covering her mouth so that her words were garbled.

But Gabe had heard and understood them. "I won't," he assured her. "I won't, that is, if you're in a truth-telling mood."

"What—what do you mean?"

"Are we going to play some more games, Pearl? Or are you ready to finally fess up to what really happened in that hotel room here in town between you and me and your man?"

"I'm going to scream."

Gabe raised a warning finger and shook it at Pearl. "Don't," he said. "If you do, it'll be the last scream you ever scream. Do you understand me?"

Pearl, her eyes wide with alarm, nodded.

"Where's the law located in this town?" Gabe asked her.

"The new deputy marshal keeps a room in the Central Hotel."

"Pearl, you and me are going to pay the deputy a visit. You're going to tell him that I killed your husband in self-defense."

"I can't. I won't. My reputation—"

"What about *my* reputation, damn it? I'm a wanted man, thanks to you and your lying. I've had bounty hunters after me because I'm wanted dead or alive, and there's a thousand-dollar price on my head. That's all because of you. Now, I don't intend to spend the rest of my life dodging bullets, so I came back here to get you to speak up and say what really happened in that hotel room where your husband died."

"I told you, my reputation—"

"Your reputation be damned!"

Before Gabe could say anything more, Pearl threw open the front door and fled from the house.

Her unexpected move took Gabe by surprise, but then he went after her, his boots pounding across the porch and down the steps. He caught her by the wrist as she was opening the gate. He pulled her close to him and said, "Now we can have a set-to right out here in the open for all your neighbors to see from behind their lace curtains, or we can go inside and settle things nice and private-like. What's it to be?"

Pearl pulled free of him and strode away, heading for the house.

Once inside again with the door closed, Gabe said, "Tell you what. Since you're so worried about your reputation, I'll make a deal with you. I'll say that it was true what you said about me forcing you to come up to my room. I'll even admit to raping you. That ought to protect your reputation.

"In exchange, you'll tell the deputy marshal that your husband threw down on me and that I had to shoot him to save my own life. Is that a bargain?"

Pearl's eyes narrowed as she considered his proposition. Finally, she said, "If I do what you want, will you go away and not bother me anymore?"

He nodded. "Now let's go."

"I'll just get my hat and gloves and my reticule. If you'll excuse me—"

Gabe followed her into the other room, unwilling to let her out of his sight. When she was ready to leave, he accompanied her out of the house and back to the Central Hotel.

The desk clerk rather huffily told Gabe, in answer to his question, that the deputy was in room nine.

When they reached the room, Gabe knocked on the door.

It was opened by a man wearing a deputy's badge.

"Don't go for your gun, Deputy," Gabe said, his colt out of its holster and aimed directly at the man. "I'm here to have a talk with you. Mrs. Rutledge has something to tell you that I'm sure you'll find real interesting. Can we come in?"

Without waiting for a response, Gabe shouldered his way past the deputy, shoving Pearl into the room before him. He closed the door and sat down in a chair.

"Have a seat, Deputy," he said. "You can start talking anytime now, Mrs. Rutledge."

Pearl looked from Gabe to the deputy and then down at the floor. Addressing the lawman, she said, "I gave the wrong impression the night my husband was killed here in the hotel."

"Wrong impression?" the deputy asked.

"This man"—she indicated Gabe with a curt nod—"killed Jerry in self-defense. It wasn't his fault. Jerry tried to kill him, and he would have if he hadn't killed Jerry first."

"But the rest of what Mrs. Rutledge said," Gabe interjected, "was all true. I did force her to come to my room with me. And I did force her to—well, you know what I'm driving at, Deputy."

The deputy glanced at Gabe and then back at Pearl. "This puts the killing of your husband in an entirely new light, Mrs. Rutledge," he remarked thoughtfully. "Yes, indeed, in an *entirely* new light."

"Now that that is settled," Pearl said with a certain primness to her tone and a fluff of her hair, "I'll be on my way. Good day to you, Deputy, Mr. Conrad."

"Wait one minute, Mrs. Rutledge," the deputy said, holding up a hand. "I want to be sure I understand this situation correctly. You say Mr. Conrad isn't guilty of murder—"

"Self-defense," Pearl said, still rather primly. "Mr. Conrad shot my husband to death while defending his own life."

"And so you don't want to testify against him in court in Fort Smith, is that what you're saying, Mrs. Rutledge?"

"That is exactly what I am saying."

"Well," the deputy said, stroking his chin as his gaze shifted from Gabe to Pearl and back again, "I reckon there's nothing to do but let you go, Mr. Conrad. If

Mrs. Rutledge won't testify against you—in fact says no crime was committed against her husband—and since there were no other witnesses to what happened in that room when Jerry Rutledge met his Maker—you're off the hook, Mr. Conrad."

Pearl, without looking at Gabe, nodded to the deputy and slipped out of the room.

As Gabe breathed a sigh of relief, the deputy said, "You're a lucky man, Conrad. I could still hold you on a charge of rape. Also kidnapping. But the lady didn't seem interested in pursuing those charges, did she?"

"There's one other matter that's on my mind, Deputy," Gabe said. "I don't know if you know it or not, but the deputy marshal who was driving that prison wagon of yours is dead. I want you to know I didn't kill him."

The lawman made a dismissive gesture. "I know all about that matter. One of the other men who rides for Judge Parker apprehended that fellow—prisoner named Rusty. He told us what happened. He said you escaped, and the deputy in charge of you brought you back and then, lo and behold, you went and escaped again. That right?"

"That's right."

"Rusty said the deputy deputized him and his pal, Charlie, and the three of them went out hunting you. Rusty said they found you, and there was some gunplay, and he shot the deputy by mistake. In the darkness, he thought the deputy was you, he said. That true, too?"

"It is."

"Well, Conrad, you're free to go."

Gabe didn't move.

"Something wrong?"

"Those dodgers that you've got plastered all over the place, Deputy. Would you see to it that they come down as fast as possible? If they don't, somebody's liable to ventilate me for the reward those dodgers offer."

"I'll get the word out on that score. Meanwhile, I'd suggest you keep your head down and your eyes on your back trail."

"I'm obliged to you, Deputy."

"Wait, I'll go with you. I'm hungry as a bear. How about you?"

"I'm not hungry. I plan to ride out of town."

Once outside, Gabe scanned the street for some sign of Pearl Rutledge. She was nowhere in sight. Just as well.

"I'll just tear this down for starters," the deputy said. He reached up and ripped a dodger down from the front wall of the hotel.

A woman who had been reading it looked at Gabe and said, "Does that mean you're not wanted any longer, Mr. Conrad?"

"You know me, ma'am?" Gabe asked her.

"The desk clerk in the hotel where I'm staying pointed you out to me when you first rode into town. He described you as a desperado. He also told me that you were wanted for murder, as that dodger indicated."

"It was all a misunderstanding, ma'am," the deputy marshal volunteered, touching the brim of his hat to her. "Mr. Conrad's not wanted by the law as of now."

"I'm sure he's relieved to know that," the woman said. And then, "Oh, dear, it's starting to snow. That will make traveling difficult."

As the deputy nodded a farewell to Gabe and the lady and walked away, Gabe said, "You're planning on doing some traveling, are you?"

The woman looked up at him—she was nearly a foot shorter than he was—and nodded. "I'm just passing through Tishomingo on my way to visit my sister in Mill Creek."

Gabe studied the woman standing before him. He noted her brown eyes that glowed with an inner warmth and her brown hair, which was as glossy as corn silk in early summer. She had an hourglass figure. Her skin was as smooth as churned butter, and her lips were full and inviting.

"You know my name," Gabe said. "What's yours?"

"Cathy Miller. Catherine Miller, actually, but my friends call me Cathy."

Hello, Cathy.

CHAPTER EIGHT

"I don't mean to sound forward, Miss Miller," Gabe said, "but I'd be pleased to buy you a cup of coffee, or maybe some ice cream or pie, or anything else that suits your fancy."

"Why, you're not being forward at all, Mr. Conrad. On the contrary, you're a most polite and obliging gentleman. I shall be pleased to accept your kind invitation."

As they headed for a nearby restaurant, Gabe was pleased to find that Cathy Miller took his arm in a firm but not overly familiar grip.

Progress.

They took a table near a window and when the waitress appeared, Gabe ordered coffee and Cathy ordered a piece of lemon meringue pie and a glass of milk.

"My mother," she said, while they waited for their order to arrive, "makes the most wonderful lemon meringue pie in the whole wide world. It melts in one's mouth, truly it does. And the meringue—it's like eating a soft summer cloud."

"How long are you staying in Tishomingo?" Gabe inquired.

Cathy looked out the window at the snow that was thickening as it continued to fall. "I don't know really. I intended to resume my journey today, actually, but now, with the snow falling, I just don't know. Perhaps I should stay put awhile longer."

"The snow's not going to last."

"It isn't? How do you know?"

"See the flakes? They're fat. Fat flakes never last. It's the little ones that last."

"You know, I think you're absolutely right. The snow isn't sticking. It's melting as soon as it hits the ground."

"Who gets the pie?" the waitress asked as she returned to the table.

"I do," Cathy said.

The pie was placed in front of her. "I know the coffee's for the gentleman," the waitress said, "so I guess this milk's yours, miss."

Cathy drew back in mild alarm as a glass of milk was plopped down on the table in front of her and some of it sloshed out onto the tablecloth.

"Good help's hard to get these days, or so I've heard," Gabe commented as the waitress, hips swinging, made her way across the room.

"I thought she was going to drown me with the milk," Cathy confided, smiling slightly.

Gabe spooned sugar from the bowl that sat in the center of the table into his cup.

"You have quite a sweet tooth, I see, Mr. Conrad. Four spoonfuls of sugar is quite a bit."

"You're right, Miss Miller, I do have a sweet tooth. I

also have a fondness for female company, which is why I'm going to take the liberty of suggesting something to you. I'm also heading north, the same as you. Why don't the two of us travel along together until you get to Mill Creek?"

Cathy busied herself with her pie. She cut off a tiny piece with her fork and daintily placed it in her mouth. She chewed, not looking at Gabe.

Finally, after swallowing, she said, "I don't know, Mr. Conrad. I'm sure your intentions are completely honest and straightforward. Aboveboard, as they say. But I'm not so sure it would be wise for me to travel alone with a gentleman such as yourself."

"Miss Miller, I assure you my intentions are honorable. I find traveling alone gets lonely, and I thought we could keep each other company. You don't need a chaperon with me, I assure you."

He continued, "I could provide you with a degree of protection, you know. It's not always safe for a woman to travel alone in Indian Territory."

"I know." Cathy hesitated a moment, and then said, "I suppose no one has to know anything about us. Why, you could be my brother, couldn't you? Or my cousin. And anyway, we don't have to explain to anyone we might happen to meet what our true relationship is. If we meet someone, and they want to think there is something improper about us traveling together, why, pshaw, we'll just let them think what they want to think."

"That's the ticket, Miss Miller," Gabe said encouragingly. "We can travel north along Pennington Creek and then cut west when we get up near Mill Creek. By the way, you do have some sort of transportation?"

"My buggy is parked in front of the hotel."

"Fine. I'll tie my dapple to the back of it and away we'll go. I can do the driving, if you like."

"Oh, I'd love it if you'd do the driving, Mr. Conrad. I *hate* driving. I'm always terrified that I'm going to lose control of my horse or that the buggy will break an axle or that something else equally dire will occur. But with a strong man like you in charge—well, I can tell just by looking at you that you'll be able to handle any emergency that might arise, though I hope none will."

Gabe drank some of his coffee. "When would you like to leave?"

"Would an hour from now be convenient? I have a few things I must pack."

"An hour from now would be fine, Miss Miller."

"Then that's all settled, Mr. Conrad."

"One thing, though."

Cathy, who had been cutting a piece of pie with her fork, looked up at Gabe. "What is that, Mr. Conrad?"

"It's this Mr. Conrad and Miss Miller business. Since the two of us are going to be traveling together, don't you think maybe we could get on a given name basis?"

"Why, yes, of course—Gabe."

More progress.

It had begun snowing again just before Gabe and Cathy Miller left Tishomingo in her buggy with his horse tied behind it.

"Maybe it won't last," Gabe said when Cathy made a worried comment about the thickness of the snow. "Let's hope it won't, anyway."

Cathy fell silent after wrapping a portion of her shawl

around the lower part of her face to protect it from the snow and the increasing cold.

"If you want, we could turn back," Gabe said to her at one point. "Wait for better traveling weather."

"I don't want to wait," she stated in an oddly flat tone. "I want to get it over and done with. I've waited long enough."

Gabe wasn't sure what she was talking about, but he supposed she was referring to her planned visit to her sister in Mill Creek.

They continued their journey with the snow thickening around them. The wind began to rise and send snow swirling across the open land and into their faces. As they passed an abandoned cabin that stood near a spring, Cathy said, "I can barely see a foot in front of my face," She paused a moment and then said, "Maybe you're right, Gabe. Maybe we should turn back and try another time."

"This storm's going to blow itself out before long," he declared. "These out-of-season storms do that. They come a'blustering and a'blowing, and then they run out of steam real fast, and before you know it, the sun's out again and the snow's starting to melt."

"Are there any settlements between here and Mill Creek?" Cathy asked him, as the buggy plowed on and the snow began to drift.

"Nope. Nothing but open land and Pennington Creek over there. Chickasaw Nation's pretty sparsely settled, at least around these parts."

Gabe knew what Cathy was thinking. She was thinking that they should find shelter somewhere. He was beginning to think she might be right. The snow was falling heavily now, and the storm showed no signs of stopping. In fact, the wind was intensifying to near blizzard-force strength.

"We'd best turn back," Gabe said decisively a few minutes later as the horse that was pulling the buggy came to a halt and stood with its head hanging down. "Your horse is about ready to throw in the towel."

"I think that's a good idea. It's grown quite cold. I feel as if I'm freezing to death."

Gabe reached out and put an arm around her. Then he clucked to the horse, slapped its rump with the reins, and turned it around. The horse moved faster now that the wind was at its back. It seemed in a hurry to get out of the storm, too.

The buggy almost rammed the horse's rump at one point when a gust of wind slammed into it and sent it scooting forward along the slippery ground. The horse balked, and it took some coaxing on Gabe's part to get it moving again. But the going was slow, too slow for his liking, because the cold was intensifying as the wind now howled across the prairie. The horse had difficulty lifting its legs out of the snow that was now several inches deep in drifts.

Gabe slapped the horse's rump again with the reins, but he could get no more speed out of the animal. It tried but failed to move any faster. A few minutes later, it came to a dead stop and nickered softly.

"What is it?" Cathy asked nervously as Gabe stepped down to the ground. "What's wrong?"

"You just sit tight right there," he told her. "I'll be back in two shakes of a lamb's tail."

He went to the horse and found what he had expected

to find. The strenuous efforts the animal had been making as it tried to pull the buggy through the snow had made it sweat profusely. Some of that sweat had dripped into its eyes and froze there, effectively blinding the horse.

Gabe blew on his hands and placed them over the animal's eyes. He repeated the process several times until the crystallized snow melted and the horse could see once again. Then he returned to where Cathy was sitting and shivering in the buggy.

"I'm going to lead your horse. I don't think he'll let himself be driven in this weather. You stay where you are."

"How far away are we from Tishomingo?"

"Not far," Gabe lied. But he saw no point in telling Cathy the truth—thay they were a good ten miles from the town. If he had done so, she would only be more worried than she obviously was right now.

He patted her on the knee and went back to the horse. He gripped its harness in one hand and began to trudge through the snow, the horse following him. He kept his eyes peeled for the goal he had set for himself, the goal that was not Tishomingo. But it was hard to see in the swirling snow, and there were no tracks to follow as he headed back the way they had come. He knew he might very well miss the destination he had set for himself. All he had to rely on were a few landmarks he had noticed along the way. The pine with the wind-sheared top which he was now passing. The hummock that rose out of the ground and sported a thick covering of chockecherry bushes on its western flank.

He was determined to make it through the blizzard, just as determined as he'd been as a fourteen-year-old boy riding through a snowstorm worse than this one to carry a warning to a neighboring Indian village that was in danger of being attacked. His journey had earned him the name Long Rider among the Oglala. If he could survive that ordeal, he could survive this.

As he walked on, straining to force the horse to follow him, he sighted the hummock in the distance and, encouraged, marched on. At last it came into sight, an apparition, dark and hulking, in the snow that was turning the world white.

He swerved and headed toward it.

"What are you doing?" Cathy called out to him, her words almost whirled away by the wind. "Are we lost?"

"We're not lost," he replied, having to shout to make himself heard over the whine of the wind. "There's a deserted cabin up ahead. See it?"

"No, I don't," Cathy replied as she squinted into the snow, blinking and wiping flakes away from her face. "Oh, yes, now I do," she cried a moment later.

When Gabe reached it, he helped Cathy down from the buggy. She sank almost knee-deep into the snow. He led her to the sagging door of the cabin, which hung on one hinge, the other having rotted completely away.

He pulled the door open and thrust her inside. Following her in, snow flying in behind him to whiten the dirt floor, he kicked the door shut and then lit a lamp that sat on the table. It gave little light because its glass globe was smoke-stained and grimy, but what light it did provide gave the dingy interior of the dusty cabin an almost cheerful appearance.

Cathy slumped into a wooden rocker. It gave way beneath her, one leg popping off it. Gabe helped her up from the floor where she had fallen in a cloud of dust.

"This place is filthy!" she exclaimed, more surprised than hurt.

"But it's a haven from the storm, filthy or not."

"Yes, thank Heaven for that. I guess I shouldn't complain."

"I'm going out."

"You're going out? Do you have to?"

"I've got to see to the horses. There's a little lean-to on the side of the cabin. I'll put them there."

"Come right back, won't you?"

"I will. While I'm gone, see what you can do about starting a fire. There's kindling in the wood box."

Gabe handed her some matches and left the cabin. Outside, he removed the harness form Cathy's horse and led it around to the lean-to, which he found contained some chopped wood and a few odd pieces of tack. He picketed the horse under the lean-to, then went and got his dapple and did the same for it.

"It's no palace," he told the animals. "But it'll do. It'll have to. It's all I got to offer you."

As he left the horses, they promptly adjusted their positions so that their heads were facing the wall of the cabin and the wind blew at their backs. Gabe hurried back inside the cabin. He was pleased to find that Cathy had a fire burning in the stone fireplace.

"All the comforts of home," he remarked as he took off his hat and slapped snow from it.

"It really isn't all that bad, is it? Some of the chinking has fallen out, but we'll just have to put up with that."

"There's rags there." Gabe pointed to a wicker sewing

basket that lay overturned on the floor. "We could stuff them in the chinks."

Cathy proceeded to do exactly that, waving Gabe into a chair. She talked as she worked. "There's coffee in the cupboard. Flour, too, but it's full of weevils. Nothing else, I'm afraid, except for some hopelessly moldy cheese."

"We won't be here long enough to get hungry."

She turned and stared at him. "You're sure about that?"

"Reasonably so, yes. This storm's bound to blow itself out before too long."

"I hope you're right. I hope that's not just wishful thinking on your part."

Gabe noted Cathy's slender ankles, which were revealed as she stretched to stuff a plaid rag in a chink above her head. He imagined what her legs must look like. Lean. Lithe. And the rest of her—all curves and twists and turns. He began to hope that the storm wouldn't blow over too soon. Not before he got a chance to get to know Cathy Miller a bit better. A *lot* better, he quickly corrected himself.

He went and got a coffeepot that sat on a counter beside the sink. He took it outside and used snow to wash it with. When it was clean, he packed it full of snow and brought it inside. When the snow it contained had melted, he proceeded to make a pot of coffee.

While it cooked in the fireplace, he took two tin cups outside and washed them with snow. Then, when the coffee had boiled, he filled the cups and handed one of them to Cathy.

"There isn't any sugar," she told him as she sat down

at a table in the center of the room. "Or cream, of course."

"I like it black."

"I can learn to."

They drank as the wind roared beyond the windows and whistled down the chimney, making the flames dance in the fireplace.

Gabe noticed that each time Cathy drank and then set her cup down on the table in front of her it clattered. He noticed, too, that her hands were unsteady. She kept glancing at the windows where the snow was piling up on the sills and at the fireplace where the flames swayed and sputtered as the wind came rushing down the chimney to chill the room.

"It will be over soon," he promised her, although he didn't know whether that was true or not.

"I keep thinking of what would have happened to me if I had set out alone," she said in a low voice. "I never would have found this place. I would have been stranded out there somewhere."

Gabe spat coffee grounds out of his mouth. "If we had any eggs, I could have used their shells to settle the grounds in the pot. I'm getting them caught between my teeth."

His attempt to take Cathy's mind off their predicament failed. She seemed not to have heard what he said.

"I probably would have frozen to death if I had been by myself," she ventured.

"Well," Gabe said, "there's no use thinking about that, is there? I mean it didn't happen. You didn't set out alone. I'm with you and you're inside and you're safe and—"

Cathy looked up at him, and he saw the anguish in her eyes. "You won't leave me here alone, will you?"

The question took him by surprise.

"Will you?" she repeated.

"No" he said, shaking his head. "I won't. What made you think I might?"

"You have your own life. You probably have places to go and things to do. You don't want to be holed up in this cabin with a woman you barely know. I wouldn't blame you if you did leave me here. After all, I am not your responsibility, am I?"

"You are for the moment, yes. And I have to say I'm glad you are."

"What do you mean?"

"Well, Cathy, I'm sure you know you cut a fine figure, and you're as pretty as any picture I've ever seen. It's no hardship for me to be around you, none whatsoever."

Cathy blushed and looked down at her hands which she had clasped in her lap.

"How come a pretty woman like yourself hasn't long since gotten herself hitched?"

Cathy looked up at him, and Gabe saw something flare in her eyes before it quickly faded away. Anger? Hate? It had been something harsh, something blunt, but it had come and gone so fast he hadn't been able to recognize it for what it was.

"I had planned to marry," she said at last. "My fiancé and I were looking forward to a long and loving life together. He was a fine man, and I loved him more than life itself. To me, he was the center of the world. He was a strong man but also gentle. At least he was with me. He came from a family of strong men, and strong women, too. His mother, before she died, raised her sons to be brave and fearless and to meet the world with a willingness to fight for what was theirs, no matter what the cost."

Gabe waited silently for Cathy to continue.

"I needed a man like my fiancé. Someone strong. I'm not a strong person myself. You just saw an example of that when I pleaded with you not to leave me alone here. I need a man to lean on. One who will shield me from the buffeting that life can give a person at times."

"You talk like it's all over between you and your man. Now, I don't mean to pry into what's clearly none of my business, but I can't help wondering what happened."

"My fiancé died."

"I'm sorry to hear that," he said sincerely.

"There won't ever be another man like him," Cathy said, as she looked away toward the nearest window and the still falling snow beyond it. "He was one of a kind."

"Maybe you shouldn't sound so sure about that. Time, it has a way of healing wounds. All kinds of wounds. I don't mean to belittle your loss. I know from what you've just told me that it must have been a heartrending one."

Cathy looked back at him. "It was."

"But, like I said, time goes on, and the pain, it may not ever go away altogether, but it does lessen. I know from my own experience." He was remembering his own wife, his Oglala wife, Yellow Buckskin Girl, killed years ago by a white cavalry captain's bullet.

"Water under the bridge."

"Beg pardon?"

"You're suggesting that what there was between my fiancé and me is now just water under the bridge."

"No, I'm not—"

"Well, you're wrong, Gabe. Dead wrong. I'll never forget him, and I'll never marry another man as long as I live, even if he were to offer me crowns and kingdoms. I will stay true to my lost love."

"Is that why you're going north to visit your sister?" Gabe asked. "To help you forget what happened?"

Cathy's eyes met his. "Perhaps."

Now what kind of an answer was that? Gabe wondered. Perhaps? He didn't get it. But he let the matter drop. He rose, went to the window, and peered out into the storm.

"Is it still bad out there?"

"It's still bad." He turned back to face Cathy.

She gazed at him expectantly.

"I had been thinking that you and me—well, that you and me, we might take this chance to get to know one another better."

Cathy's eyes grew cold.

"But that was before I found out you were in mourning," Gabe said.

"You intend to take advantage of me," Cathy accused.

"I intend no such thing. I just thought—"

"You thought you had me exactly where you wanted me. You thought you could have your way with me and there would be nothing I could do to stop you."

"Cathy, you got me all wrong. I'm a man. You're a woman and a desirable one. What I'm feeling—what I want—look, you don't have to do a thing you don't want to do. I thought you knew that."

"You're lying, of course."

"I'm not."

Cathy gave a cracked little laugh. "That's why you agreed to accompany me in the first place, isn't it? So somewhere at sometime you could possess me?"

"I'm willing to admit that I thought from the minute I first laid eyes on you that I wouldn't mind making love to you. But, no, that's not why I offered to ride along with you. I told you, trails traveled alone are lonely trails. That's the main reason I offered to go with you as far as Mill Creek."

Cathy turned her back on him.

"I'm real sorry you read me wrong. I think it might be better if I left now. I don't want you all skittish and fidgety simply because I'm around and you figure you'd better be on your guard all the time to keep me from defiling you."

Gabe turned and went to the door. Before he could open it, Cathy ran to it and prevented him from doing so. She threw her arms around his neck and kissed him passionately on the lips.

Her actions had taken him totally by surprise. One minute she had been accusing him of dishonorable intentions and the next here she was in his arms.

As their lips parted, Cathy looked up at him and said, "I couldn't help myself. I want you Gabe. I want you now."

"But you said—"

"Never mind what I said. That was all bombast. I felt I had to say those things or else you would think me wanton. But when you threatened to leave me—I couldn't let you go."

"I'm glad you didn't. I wasn't all that eager to go out in this storm and away from a lovely lady like yourself."

"The truth of the matter is I've been wanting you all along. You're a handsome man, Gabe. Any woman would have felt the way I did—the way I do. It's nothing to be ashamed of. It's simply natural, isn't it?"

If you say so, Gabe thought, and eagerly kissed Cathy.

CHAPTER NINE

The storm ended two days later. The sun came out and shone brightly on the snow that covered the ground, the trees, the rocks, and half of the cabin where Gabe and Cathy were, in effect, prisoners since they could not get the door open. Snow lay banked against it, blown there by the wind.

Though Gabe pushed against the door with all his might, he could just barely budge it. Despite his strenuous efforts, he managed to force it open only an inch. Even with Cathy's help, he could open it no more than that one tantalizing inch through which sunlight filtered slightly to brighten the interior of the cabin.

"We've got to get out of here," Cathy said in a strained voice. "If we don't, we'll starve to death."

Gabe knew she was right. He also knew that in time the sun would melt the snow. But how much of it? And how quickly?

"We've got two choices," he told Cathy after pondering the matter in silence for some time. "The way I see it is, we can stay put and hope that the sun hurries up and melts most of the snow, or we can try to make it back to Tishomingo, snow or no snow."

"That's a truly terrible choice," Cathy groaned.

Gabe nodded. She was right. "You got a better idea?" He asked the question, not mockingly, but in the faint hope that she might indeed have one.

She didn't.

He made another pot of coffee with the grounds left from the previous pot, since they had run out of fresh coffee the day before. When it was ready, he sat with Cathy at the table, and they both drank some of it in an oppressive silence. That silence became even more oppressive as they both noticed the sunlight that streamed through the cabin's window begin to fade.

Cathy suddenly leapt to her feet, overturning her chair as she did so, and ran to the window. She peered out and then let out a cry that reminded Gabe of one a wild animal caught in a trap might make.

From where he sat, he could see what had torn that cry from her. The sky was clouding up. It was swiftly turning from bright blue to dull gray.

Cathy, at the window, went rigid as the first flakes of snow began to flutter down from the clouds.

"Your coffee's getting cold." Gabe said, in an attempt to distract her.

"*Damn* the coffee!" she cried, whirling around to face him. "What are we going to do now that it's started snowing again?"

He rose and went to her. Placing both hands on her trembling shoulders, he said softly, "I told you the two choices I was able to come up with."

"Do you think, if we tried, we could make it back to Tishomingo?"

"We won't know till we do try, will we?"

"Will the horses be able to make it? The snow has drifted deep in places."

"Maybe we should sit tight for another few hours. Maybe for one more day."

"*No!*" The word burst forth from Cathy's lips. "I don't want to starve to death. We've got to get out of here."

"I could go out hunting, though game goes to ground in bad weather like this. I'm not likely to find anything."

Cathy shook her head.

"I couldn't stand it if you left me here alone. No, we've got to try to get out of here together. We can help each other."

Gabe wasn't sure how much help Cathy would or could be to him out there in that white wasteland beyond the cabin's door. He also wasn't sure how much help he could be to her when the going got really rough, and it would, he knew, long before they covered the ten miles that lay between the cabin and the town of Tishomingo.

Forcing a cheerfulness into his voice which he did not feel, he said, "Let's give it a try."

Before Cathy could change her mind, he made himself ready for the journey that lay ahead of them by bundling himself up as warmly as he could. He told Cathy to do the same. Then he picked up a coil of rope that hung from a nail on the wall and went over to the window. He put a fist through it. Brushing away the shards of glass that remained in the frame and the snow from the sill, he turned to Cathy.

Placing his hands together and interlocking his fingers, he formed a saddle into which, at a nod from him, she stepped. He boosted her up and helped her climb out through the window. Then he followed her, taking the same path to the outside world.

They stood in a drift that nearly reached their hips and looked gravely at one another. Then Gabe began to plow through the drift, his hand gripping Cathy's, as he headed around the side of the cabin to where he had left the horses in the lean-to.

When they reached the horses, he turned to Cathy and said, "We'll never make it using the buggy. It'll get bogged down real fast. You can ride my horse."

"What about you?"

"I'll ride your horse."

"Bareback?"

"Sure." Gabe almost smiled, thinking of all the times he had ridden bareback while growing up among the Oglala.

He freed both horses and helped Cathy board his dapple. After looping one end of the rope he had taken from the cabin firmly around the neck of his horse, he sprang aboard the other one and moved out. He had to give the rope several sharp tugs to get his horse to move out into the blinding snow, but at last it did.

They moved slowly through the drifts, neither of them speaking because they quickly found that when they tried to do so, snow and wind flew into their mouths and made speech virtually impossible.

They had traveled for more than an hour when Gabe held up a hand to call a halt. Both he and Cathy sat their horses then, letting the animals rest and get their breath.

The horse under Gabe was heaving as it breathed, its barrel expanding and contracting at a rapid rate.

" . . . move on!"

He heard only the last two words Cathy had shouted into the wind. He ignored her. This was no time and these were no conditions under which to try to explain to her that he had to think first of the horses' welfare. If she said anything more, he didn't hear it.

At last, they resumed their journey, moving with agonizing slowness through the storm. The sky above them was invisible. The ground below them was a monotonous stretch of unrelieved whiteness. At one point, Gabe again called a halt. He dismounted and removed ice crystals which were forming on both horses' eyes, making it difficult for them to see. Once back in the saddle, he noticed that small icicles were forming on the mane of his mount as it sweated and its sweat froze, matting the animal's hair. The icicles grew larger as the journey grew longer. His mount nickered as one of the icicles broke free by virtue of its weight and ripped hair and skin from the animal's neck, leaving a bare bloody spot behind.

Time began to lose its meaning for Gabe. He had no sure sense any longer of what time of day it was. The world around him was a blend of white and gray, the landscape gradually becoming almost featureless as the snow hid portions of it.

He glanced over his shoulder from time to time to make sure that Cathy was all right. She sat hunched in the saddle, her hands gripping the saddle horn, her head bowed, the straps of her reticule looped about her wrist. He wondered if she would make it. He wondered if he would make it. He vowed both of them would. Again he thought of that long-ago ride through the snow. He intended to do everything humanly possible to see to it that they both arrived safely in Tishomingo.

Sometime later, as he rode with his eyes closed against the storm, opening them only briefly from time to time to make certain he was still on course, he felt the horse under him change its gait. It seemed to have stumbled, but he couldn't be sure about that because of the depth of the snow. He leaned to one side and looked down at the coating of ice that had formed on its lower legs.

There was nothing to do, he decided, but to give the animal another rest. He slid out of the saddle and stood for a moment, getting his footing. Then he went back to where Cathy had brought his dapple to a halt as well. He untied the rope from around the dapple's neck and then tied it around the neck of the other horse. He went and got a grip on the bridle of his own dapple and led it up in front of the other horse. He tied the free end of the rope to his dapple's tail. When he was satisfied that it was knotted securely, he began to lead his horse with Cathy aboard it through the storm, the other one trailing behind.

He was keenly aware as he walked that Cathy had not attempted to question his actions. Was that a sign that she was so beaten down by the storm that she no longer cared what happened? He didn't let himself speculate any further in that direction, but he did keep looking over his shoulder from time to time to make sure she was still in the saddle.

He guessed that they had managed to cover another mile when he was brought up short as the rope in his hand grew suddenly taut. He turned and saw what had happened. Cathy's horse, trailing behind his own, had gone down in a drift. He went to it and tried to get it up on its feet again. After a few minutes, he gave up the effort, convinced the horse would move no more.

Cathy stared dully at him as he drew his revolver. She continued staring, no emotion evident on her face, as he shot the horse.

He untied the rope that had bound it to his dapple, coiled it, and dropped it over his saddle horn. Then he trudged on through the swirling snow that was finding its way into his nostrils, his eyes, and his open mouth as he panted onward. They had not gone far when Cathy let out a shrill cry.

Gabe turned and saw her slide out of the saddle and begin whirling about in the snow like a woman gone wild.

"What's wrong?" he yelled to her. When she didn't answer him but continued moving frantically about in the deep snow, he went to her and seized her by the shoulders. "What's wrong?" he repeated.

When she didn't answer him but tried instead to break free of him, he shook her until her teeth rattled.

She seemed then to come to her senses, but her eyes still darted about. "My reticule," she gasped. "It must have slipped off my wrist. I've lost it."

Gabe relaxed. "Forget it," he told her.

"No!" she cried, shaking her head furiously from side to side. "I've got to find it."

"You'll never find it in these drifts," he pointed out. "Come on and let's get out of here."

Cathy stubbornly resisted. When he reached for her, intending to get her back into the saddle of his dapple, she drew back. When he took a step toward her, she began to pummel him with her small fists.

All this, he thought, standing his ground under her onslaught, for a woman's handbag. Maybe she's got her life's savings tucked away in it. Maybe that's why she's so hell-bent on finding it now when we're caught out in the open in the middle of a brutal snowstorm.

He seized her wrists. For a moment, they both stood there staring into each other's eyes through the curtain of snowflakes separating them. Then Cathy began to weep forlornly. She simply stood where she was and let the tears roll down her cheeks, making almost no sound as she wept.

Gabe finally gave in. "All right," he said, "I'll look for your reticule."

Cathy's eyes widened with delight like those of a child given a long-wanted gift.

"I'll help you," she said and began to move about again, her eyes scanning the surface of the snow into which her feet sank.

Gabe walked back the way they had come, his head lowered against the wind, his eyes searching for any sign of the lost reticule. He saw none and didn't expect to see any. The snow, with the help of the wind, had probably buried the handbag by now.

"Gabe!"

He turned at the sound of Cathy calling his name. He could hardly see her. She was just a grayish figure standing in the storm beside a bulkier and equally grayish figure—his dapple.

"Gabe," she cried again, and there was unrestrained joy in her voice. "I've found it!"

He made his way back to where she stood, her hands held out in front of her, and when he arrived at her side, he saw that she was cupping her reticule in her outstretched hands.

"I saw this hole," she told him breathlessly. "It was like a little burrow in the snow. I reached down into it and—voilà, there it was." She looked down at her recovered reticule, a broad smile on her face.

"I'm glad you found it," he told her. "Now, let's move on."

When she was in the saddle once again, her precious handbag looped around her wrist, he got a grip on the dapple's bridle and they moved out.

Twenty minutes later, a shaft of sunlight broke through the gray sky and white snow. It immediately disappeared.

Gabe stopped and looked up at the sky.

"Is it ending?" Cathy piped nervously from behind him. "Do you think the storm is finally coming to an end?"

He didn't know and said so.

They had resumed their journey when Cathy cried out and pointed to a break in the clouds through which a small patch of pale blue sky could be seen. Gabe saw it and willed it to widen.

Ten minutes later only an occasional stray flake of snow drifted lazily down out of the rapidly clearing sky. The sun now shone brightly.

Gabe chose to follow a circuitous route toward their destination of Tishomingo, moving in the depressions between tall banks of snow that had been made by the wind. They took him to the left, to the right, to the left again. He knew it would take them longer to get where they were going in this fashion but, more importantly, he also knew that it would place far less strain on his dapple. To ease the journey even more for the horse, he stopped every ten minutes and insisted that Cathy get down out of the saddle while the horse rested. Otherwise, he explained to her, the animal would drop dead of exhaustion.

"The sun—it's so wonderful to see it again!" she enthused during one of their rest stops. "But it is absolutely blinding the way it's reflected by the snow."

"That's the kind of thing that can lead to snow blindness."

"Oh, dear."

"It's only temporary, but you can't see a thing while it lasts. You're as good as born blind when it happens to you."

Concern spread across Cathy's face.

Gabe took his tin container of matches from his pocket and struck one on the seat of his jeans. He let it burn halfway down and then blew it out. He rubbed it on the skin beneath his eyes, blackening it.

"Whatever are you doing?" Cathy inquired curiously as she watched him.

"It cuts down on the glare," he explained, and then proceeded to use burnt matches to blacken the skin beneath both of her eyes.

She laughed when he had finished and declared, "I must look an absolute fright."

"You won't win any beauty contests looking like you do at the moment, but you also won't lose your eyesight."

He helped her climb back into the saddle, and they rode out again. Cathy cried out in mild alarm when a shower of melting snow fell from a thick tree limb and landed squarely on top of her and the dapple's head.

It took them another hour of traveling before they caught their first glimpse of Tishomingo sprawled in the distance. The buildings in town had snow piled high on their roofs, and the streets were clogged with it.

"We're just about there," Gabe commented as he plowed on through the snow, his legs beginning to ache with the effort he had been making for what seemed to him to have been an eternity.

"Stop," Cathy said.

He didn't.

"I said stop."

"I thought you were anxious to get to town."

"I am. But there is something I must do first."

He glanced over his shoulder at Cathy and then stopped dead in his tracks when he saw the snub-nosed version of Colt's Peacemaker .45, sometimes called the Shopkeeper's Model, in her hand. The gun was aimed directly at him.

He looked from it to Cathy's face. Her lips formed a thin, grim line. Her eyes were icy. Her jaw was set.

"What's this all about?" he asked her, frowning.

"I can make it on my own from here," she replied. She stepped down from the saddle to face Gabe.

"Well," he said, "if that's the way you feel, you're welcome to do so. Only I don't know what's got into you—"

"Hate's got into me," she interrupted stonily.

"I don't understand, Cathy. What—"

"I would have done this long ago. I planned to do it once we were well away from Tishomingo, but then the snow started to fall and I wasn't sure I could manage on my own. Then things got even worse, and I was sure I couldn't. So I was forced to postpone my plan."

"What plan is that?"

"Throw your gun down."

When Gabe hesitated, Cathy practically screamed at him, repeating her order at the top of her voice.

He unshucked his revolver and tossed it into the snow, where it sank out of sight between him and Cathy.

"Speaking of guns," he said evenly, "I take it you had that one stashed away in that reticule of yours. Which is why you got so all-fired upset about losing it before. Am I right?"

"You're right."

"You mentioned a plan you had. What is it?"

"I'm going to kill you," Cathy stated bluntly.

"Why?"

"Why?" she repeated mockingly. "Because you killed the man I loved with all my heart and soul, *that's* why!"

Gabe's thoughts were racing. Which one, he asked himself, as he kept his gaze trained on Cathy. Archie Hoover or Jerry Rutledge? He was sure that this woman who looked ready and indeed eager to shoot him was connected in some way with one of the two men he had killed. She had spoken of hate. Hate was a cousin of revenge, he knew very well.

"You killed my Archie," Cathy accused coldly, answering the question that had been in Gabe's mind. "Archie and I were planning to marry."

Gabe recalled having been told by Oren Hoover that Archie had been about to marry. So this woman with the gun was to have been Archie's wife. They would have made a good pair, Gabe decided ruefully.

"I went to pieces when Caleb Hoover came and told me that he had gone out after you," Cathy continued. "He told me he and Oren had gone to Denton looking for Archie when he failed to meet them when and where they had planned. That's where they learned about the run-in you had with Archie in the Alhambra Saloon. The doctor in Denton told them, when they were asking around about Archie, about you. He told them your name and described you. He said you had ridden out after Archie, intending to kill him for stabbing your friend."

"Your best beloved had no right to do that," Gabe said bluntly. "My friend wasn't harming him in any way."

Cathy dismissed Gabe's words with an impatient toss of her head. "Caleb said he had sent Oren out to find and kill you. But, when Oren didn't return, Caleb decided Oren might be in trouble and in need of help, so he rode out to find him—and Archie, too. It was some time before I saw Caleb again. When I did, he told me the terrible news that he had found Archie's corpse, and then he'd caught up with you, and you admitted killing Archie, and Oren as well. Caleb said he vowed to avenge his sons' death, but you nearly killed him and he barely managed to escape from you by the skin of his teeth."

"Where's the old man now?"

"I don't know. When I last talked to him and learned that he had failed in his mission, I made up my mind right then and there to do what the Hoover menfolk had failed to do."

"Namely, track me down and kill me."

"That's exactly right, yes. I thought, at one point, that I, too, was going to fail in my self-appointed task. I got as far as Tishomingo, where I learned that you had killed another man."

"Jerry Rutledge. I killed him in self-defense."

"I was told you had been taken to Fort Smith in Arkansas to stand trial there for that killing. I didn't think I could get you away from the law and kill you as I planned to do. I stayed in Tishomingo while trying to decide on my next move. The only thing I knew for sure was that I couldn't give up, not when I'd come so far and you had ruined my life when you killed the man that had given it meaning.

"As fortune would have it, my decision was made for me when you showed up in Tishomingo with that woman."

"Pearl Rutledge."

"The desk clerk in the hotel pointed you out to me. I saw you go to talk to the deputy marshal. I stood in front of that dodger that described you and the killing of Jerry Rutledge and then—well, the rest you know."

"Somebody might happen along and see you do what you're planning to do," Gabe said, not believing what he had said for a minute, but trying to stall Cathy while he sought a way out of the desperate and very dangerous situation he found himself in.

"No one will be out and about in this snow," Cathy said, almost gleefully. "And now that I can manage to get to Tishomingo by myself, I can do what I've been intending to do ever since we first met."

"When you and I were together back in that cabin—" Gabe began, still stalling.

But Cathy interrupted him, contemptuously. "That— *you*—were disgusting!"

"I thought you enjoyed yourself. You sure did seem to at the time."

"I *pretended* to. What else could I do? If I refused you, you probably would have walked out on me, and I needed your help to get back to civilization. It was just part of the game I had to play, however unpleasant it might be. I simply did what I knew I had to do."

Gabe took a step in Cathy's direction. "Let me tell you what happened in the showdown between Archie and me." He took another step toward her.

"Stay back!" she cried, brandishing her gun.

"We tangled," Gabe said, standing his ground, "and a gun went off and Archie got killed."

"I don't want to hear *stories*!" Cathy cried, her voice shrill.

"I didn't kill him in cold blood," Gabe said, edging still closer to her.

"Get back!"

Cathy's words were barely out of her mouth when Gabe kicked snow in her direction. It flew up into the air and struck her in the face. She gave a startled cry and staggered backward. Then she went down, and as she did so, her gun fired reflexively.

Gabe was upon her instantly. He tried to wrest the revolver from her hand, but her grip on it was like iron and he failed to do so. Unwilling to strike a woman, he continued tussling with her. She struck him on the side of the head with the barrel of her weapon.

The blow momentarily stunned him.

In that brief moment, Cathy scurried out from under him and ran panting to a spot some distance away.

As she turned back toward Gabe, leveling her gun at him, he leapt to his feet and ran as fast as he could through the drifts and up the side of the nearby mountain. If he could just get to higher ground, he would have a better chance of avoiding being killed.

He ran a zigzag course, falling twice in the snow. He took cover behind a tree, his back pressed tightly against it, and sucked in great gulps of cold air. More shots sounded. One of them tore bark from the tree he was hiding behind.

The sound of the shots Cathy had fired at him reverberated loudly in the still air.

He considered leaving his cover and heading higher. Maybe he could get out of range of Cathy's gun. He was about to make another run for it when he heard a sound like thunder. The sound hadn't been made by gunfire. Then—what? He stood stock-still, listening to the sound that was not quite like any he had ever heard before. Then, as he stood there, he felt the ground shift beneath his feet.

No, not the ground. The snow. The wet snow that was hard-packed under his boots as it began to melt.

He looked out from his cover and saw Cathy reloading her revolver. Then she started up the sloping side of the mountain toward him, her gun aimed in his direction, a determined and deadly expression on her pinched face. He ducked back behind the tree.

Gone now was the lovely woman he had bedded. A vengeful witch stood in her place down there below him.

Again she fired.

Again he felt the snow cover shift beneath his boots.

The sound came again. A rumbling, like thunder.

Cathy gave a strangled cry.

Gabe peered out at her from behind the tree trunk.

A thick mist of snow was flying through the air. Then the snow that covered the slope began to slide toward Cathy and toward his horse. She threw up her hands and screamed. His horse fled. The snow roared relentlessly on as the avalanche caused by the vibrations of Cathy's shots tore down the side of the mountain toward her.

Cathy turned and ran to the right, the deep snow underfoot slowing her progress. The sliding snow caught up with her. It completely covered her and then roared and rumbled on as it continued pursuing its downward course.

Gabe stepped out from behind the tree he had been holding onto tightly to keep from being swept away and went slipping and sliding down the slope toward the spot where he had last seen Cathy. He knew he was taking a risk. He knew she would kill him if he gave her half a chance. But he couldn't let her remain buried beneath the awful weight of the avalanche. He had to try to save her.

He reached the spot where she had vanished and dropped down on his knees. Frantically, he began to dig in the snow with his bare hands. Snow flew in all directions. Minutes later, he uncovered a hand. He continued digging. Cathy's face appeared.

Her eyes were open. Her skin was blue. She had suffocated beneath the crushing weight of the snow that had so swiftly and completely covered her.

Gabe got up and trudged back to where Cathy had first confronted him. He dug through the snow for some time until he finally found his .44. He holstered it and headed for his horse, which had escaped the avalanche.

CHAPTER TEN

As Gabe walked into Tishomingo leading his dapple, he saw few people on the street because of the heavy snowfall, but one he saw and recognized greeted him cheerfully.

"You're back in town?" the deputy marshal he had met earlier called to him from a boardwalk that had been cleared of snow in front of a dry goods store. "Or didn't you leave yet?"

"I left. Didn't get far. Got snowbound in an abandoned cabin me and the lady I was traveling with found."

"Lady? That wouldn't be the lady I left you talking to about your dodger, now, would it?"

"That's who it was. I intended to look you up, but now that we've met . . . The lady's dead, Deputy."

The lawman frowned. "Dead, you say? Conrad, you do seem to spend a lot of time with people who wind up deceased."

"Before your suspicioning gets to galloping, Deputy," Gabe said, somewhat testily, "let me hurry up and tell you that the lady—her name was Cathy Miller—

got killed in an avalanche that went sliding down that mountain you got yonder outside of town. I didn't have a hand in her dying.

"I'd have brought her in on my horse, but he's about done in. I reckon you'll want to fetch her down from the mountain when you get the chance and see that she gets a decent burial."

"What'd you say her name was?"

"Miller. Cathy Miller. The Cathy's short for Catherine, she told me."

"From a little town named Corliss down across the Texas border? You're talking about *that* Cathy Miller?"

"She didn't tell me where she hailed from. You knew her Deputy?"

"No, but there were some gents who rode into town just before the snowstorm hit, they knew her all right. They were asking around about her, asking had anybody seen her. They asked me had I seen her, as a matter of fact. I told them I didn't know if I had or not. I told them I'd never met up with any woman named Cathy Miller."

"How many gents are you talking about, Deputy?"

"Oh, there was a whole flock of them."

"You know their names, by any chance?"

"The fella who seemed to be leading the bunch—the one who did most of the talking—said his name was Caleb Hoover."

Gabe stiffened at the sound of the name. "Where are these men now?" he asked.

"They were fixing to ride out of town, but then the storm hit. So they stayed on. They're at the Central Hotel."

"I'm obliged to you, Deputy," Gabe said. He began to lead his dapple down the street, walking on one of the ragged tracks left behind by a wagon that had obviously been driven by some intrepid soul through the deep snow.

So Caleb Hoover was back again. Hoover keeps showing up like a bad penny, Gabe thought. He had intended to rent a room in the Central Hotel until most of the snow melted and traveling would be easier. But that was now out of the question since Hoover and the men with him were there at the hotel.

He made his way to the livery barn. A path had been shoveled from the street to its door. He entered the building and was greeted by the farrier, who was working at his forge just inside the door.

"Help you, mister?" the man inquired, as he continued pounding a red-hot horseshoe he was holding in his fire with a pair of tongs.

"My horse is about done in. Half dead, as a matter of fact. I need to have him rubbed down good, fed, and watered. I also need a place where I can hole up for a few hours until he's fit to travel again."

The farrier looked up from his fire. "Hole up? What about the Central Hotel? There's another hotel in town, too, named the—"

"I'd like to stay inside your stable, if that's all right with you."

Gabe withdrew a gold eagle from a pocket of his jeans and held it out to the farrier.

The man looked down at it and then up at Gabe.

"That's on top of whatever you're going to charge me for seeing to my horse and for letting me bed down in your livery stable," Gabe told him.

The farrier put down his hammer and took the money. Pocketing it, he pointed to a dim room beyond an open door.

"That there's my tack room," he declared. "You can hole up in there if you like."

"I'm much obliged to you. I'm in dire need of some shut-eye."

Gabe went into the room that had been pointed out to him. It smelled of leather mixed with the odor of manure from the main part of the livery stable. As he closed the door and kicked some old straw into a corner to serve as a makeshift bed, dust rose from it, making him sneeze.

He lay down, folded his arms, closed his eyes, and was asleep within seconds.

Water and words.

Gabe awoke to the sound of both. Water dripping. Words being spoken beyond the closed door of the tack room.

He lay without moving, listening, all his senses alert.

Water was dripping from the eaves of the livery stable. Through a knothole in the plank wall of the room, weak sunlight filtered.

I slept through the night, he thought, surprised. He listened to the male voices coming from beyond the closed door of the tack room.

There were two of them. One harsh and guttural and one almost amiable, the latter belonging to the farrier.

"You said you'd pay," the farrier said.

"Two dollars tops," the other man said.

Silence then.

Too much silence.

Gabe got up and flattened himself against the wall opposite the tack room's door. In his hand was his Colt, cocked and ready for firing.

There was a knock on the door.

"Who's out there?" Gabe barked.

"Me."

Gabe recognized the farrier's voice.

"What do you want?"

"Your horse is sick. I want to know what you want to do about it."

Gabe, gun still in his hand, went to the door and eased it open a crack. He peered out into the larger room and saw no one other than the farrier. Horses stood in stalls, his dapple one of them. Dust motes drifted in rays of sunlight streaming through the wide open outer door of the livery barn.

"Put that gun away," the farrier said. "Guns make me nervous."

"What's wrong with my horse?" Gabe asked, holstering his gun.

"Looks a lot like colic to me. He's having spasms."

"I'll take a look at him. If it's not too bad, I'll give him a dose of sweet milk and molasses."

Gabe went to the stall where his dapple was housed and, after eyeing the horse, he looked back at the farrier, who was on his way to the outer door.

"He hasn't got colic," Gabe called out to the man. "He's not trying to scratch his belly and he's not the least bit fidgety. What made you think—"

The farrier ducked out the door and disappeared.

A man rose up from behind the wall of a nearby stall. His gun appeared above the wall. He fired at Gabe.

But Gabe, the instant the man's gun hand had come into sight, had moved to position himself behind one of the uprights supporting the livery stable's roof. The man's shot whistled harmlessly past him.

Gabe held his fire. "Who the hell are you?" he yelled.

"My name's Ed Darby. I'm going to kill you, Conrad."

"Listen, Darby. I'm not a wanted man anymore. That matter's over and done with. I—"

"You're wanted by me and mine."

"I'm trying to tell you there's no price on my head. So if you and yours are bounty hunters and you kill me, you're going to find out that all you did was waste lead. I'm not wanted anymore."

The man fired a second shot that ate its way into the upright Gabe was standing behind.

"Go ask the deputy marshal in town, Darby. He'll tell you I'm speaking the truth."

"You got me all wrong," Darby said.

"Then set me right."

"I come in here just now to get my horse. The fellows siding me, they're still asleep, most of them over to the hotel. The farrier, he told me you were in that tack room back there. That's because he wanted the money we promised to pay for any information about you, Conrad."

"Look, you're wasting your time."

"We don't give a shit about you killing that Rutledge fellow. That's not why we want you. It ain't for the bounty they put on your head over that Rutledge killing.

It's for what you did to our kin."

"You say your name is Darby. I take it you're kin of the Hoovers. Am I right?"

"You're right, yes, sir, you surely are. Me, I was first cousin to Archie and Oren Hoover. Their pa's my ma's brother."

Gabe drew a deep breath and slowly let it out. He glanced at the open door of the livery stable. He could see water running down the street in the ruts made by wagon wheels as the sun grew hotter and the snow melted.

"There's more of us than just me," Darby bragged. "There's Caleb Hoover, of course. Archie and Oren's daddy? Sure, you know him all right. He almost got you once when he went after you all by his lonesome. But it seems like he needed help, which is why he made the rounds of his relatives. There's uncles and nephews and some cousins, who've been hunting you, Conrad. And now, by God, *I* found you!"

"Finding's not the same as killing," Gabe pointed out.

"You're as good as dead right this minute, Conrad."

Maybe, Gabe thought. Maybe not. He swung his arm out around the upright and squeezed off a shot.

Darby's gun hand disappeared. Darby himself was silent. Then he scooted out from behind the wall of the stall and too cover behind another one that was nearer to Gabe. He fired again, but the shot was too high because Gabe had squatted down behind the upright.

"What the hell's going on in here?"

Gabe glanced over his shoulder and saw Caleb Hoover standing in the doorway of the livery stable.

"Uncle Caleb," Darby cried excitedly, "it's Conrad! I got him him pinned down!"

A broad smile appeared on Hoover's face. He drew his gun, but before he could get off a single round, Gabe fired at him, forcing him to leap to the side and take cover behind the stable's wall.

From that position, he continued firing at Gabe. From his position behind the stall, so did Darby.

"We've got you now!" Caleb yelled. "The fox is finally run to ground by us hounds!" he gloated and fired again.

Gabe returned the fire, and then the hammer of his gun clicked on an empty chamber. He quickly reloaded. He could hear Darby doing the same.

Gabe reached out and took down a short length of rope that was looped over a tenpenny nail driven into the upright. His gaze drifted to the dapple and his saddle and bridle draped over the wall of the dapple's stall. His gaze then shifted to where Darby had taken cover, and then to the open door and Caleb Hoover, who was hidden to the left of it. He thoughtfully gauged the distance between himself and the horse, tried to figure how long it would take him to cover that distance. He wondered if Darby or Hoover might be able to drill him before he could get safely inside the dapple's stall. They might be able to, he calculated. Let's see if they can, he thought, and ran like hell.

Shots resounded in the stable, splintering wooden walls and kicking up clouds of dust when they plowed into bales of hay stacked against one wall.

As Gabe looped the length of rope in his hand around the lower jaw of his dapple to form a war bridle like those used by the Oglala during battle, he saw the stable's doorway darken as men came running up to it. He counted five men. Then, at a shouted warning from Hoover, all five of them ducked out of the doorway.

Could he do it? Did he dare try to do it now that there were six men with killing on their minds outside the livery? There was only one way to find out.

But before Gabe could put his plan into action, Hoover yelled, "I've got Cousin Ace Everett out here now, Conrad. Also my nephew, Jubal Bates. Jubal's just fifteen, but he's a crack shot. He can shoot the eye out of a fly at fifty paces. So can his older brother, Abel. I rounded up all the menfolk in the family to come after you, Conrad," Hoover concluded, and then a volley of shots from him and his kinfolk exploded in a deafening barrage of sound.

Gabe didn't return the fire. He waited until it stopped and then, bracing himself, his body primed for action, he sprang onto the back of the dapple and, guiding it by means of the war bridle he had fashioned, sent it galloping through the open door of the livery stable.

Shots from Darby followed him. All of them missed him, but some came far too close for comfort. A fusillade of gunfire followed him as he galloped away from the livery stable and down the street, hunkering down low against his horse's neck and withers to make himself less of a target.

He turned his horse, heading for an alley that would get him out of the line of fire. He almost made it to the alley when a round fired by one of his attackers slammed into the horse's head.

The dapple went down like a dropped stone, throwing

Gabe, who tumbled head over heels through the snow and the mud in the street.

The men at the livery stable whooped in triumph as they continued firing at him. He squirmed along the ground until he reached the alley, his body aching, particularly his left shoulder, which had hit the ground hard when he had fallen from his dapple.

Once behind the wall of a building, he knelt and, gripping his .44 in both hands, fired at the men who were all racing toward him. He brought one of them down. He guessed he had hit Jubal Bates, judging by the age of his target. He turned and ran down the alley and up a pair of steps leading to the second story. At the top of the steps, he found a door, but it was locked. He stepped back and then slammed his right shoulder against it. When the door didn't give in, he repeated the tactic. On his third try, the door swung open, its jamb splintered into fragments.

He hurried inside and found himself in a warehouse where crates and boxes were piled high along the walls and in the center of the floor. In the dim light seeping through several dirty windows, he maneuvered his way to the front of the building. He looked out onto the street through one of the windows.

They were down below him—six men racing toward the building where he had taken cover. A seventh man— the one he had shot—lay sprawled in the mud farther up the street, his arms flung out, his face turned to the sky.

Gabe threw up the window's sash and took aim, his gun hand moving swiftly as he tracked the men who were running after him. He fired once. One of the men spun in a circle as the round practically lifted him off his feet. Then he went down, blood spurting from his throat to mix with the mud beneath him. He tried to speak, but no words would come.

Gabe fired at him again, and this time he finished the job.

The rest of the men returned his fire as they simultaneously scrambled for cover of some kind. He took careful note of each man's position, mentally cataloging all of them. One was down behind a wooden water trough diagonally across the street. Another was in an alley. A third was down behind a water barrel that stood beneath a rooftop spout. Two other men—Caleb Hoover and Ed Darby—were hidden behind the trunks of two sycamores growing at the end of the boardwalk where the main street gave way to grass.

A staccato series of shots were fired at Gabe, who ducked away from the window and stood with his back flattened against the wall to the right of the window. He waited a moment and then stepped up to the window, took one quick look, and fired.

He got one of the men in the leg, the one who had taken refuge in the alley. Not good enough. He fired a quick shot, and this time his round tore into the same man's chest, killing him instantly. The man pitched forward and lay still in the street, his gun still in his hand, still faintly smoking.

"Caleb, the son of a bitch has done for Jubal and Lester Cooley and Cousin Everett," the man behind the water trough yelled. "He's done for damn near half of us, and the bastard's still alive and kicking!"

"You've got to learn to look on the bright side of

things, Abel," Hoover responded. "There's still more than half of us left. There's you. There's me. There's Ed Darby. And there's Cousin Kane over there behind that water barrel. *We're* all still alive and kicking, too!"

Caleb fired at the window on the second floor. His round went through the aperture and fell to the floor inside.

"We'll get him," Caleb boasted, as if trying to disguise the fact that the shot he had just fired had done Gabe no harm. "We'll clean Conrad's plow, just you wait and see if we don't!"

Gabe left the window and ran back through the building. When he reached the rear of the building, he climbed out a window and, standing on the sill, reached up and got a grip He holstered his revolver and then reached up with his other hand. On the roof with one hand. Slowly, grunting, he hauled himself up onto the flat, tar paper roof. He ran to the front of the building, drawing his .44 as he went, and hunkered down behind the parapet there.

Down below him, from their respective positions, two of the four surviving Hoover clan were still firing at the spot where he had been on the second floor—Caleb Hoover and Ed Darby.

But where were Abel Bates and the man Hoover had identified as Cousin Kane? Both men had vanished.

Gabe scanned the streets and the rooftops opposite him, but saw no sign of the pair. He glanced behind him. Nothing. His attention was drawn back to the sycamore trees and Hoover and Darby, firing at the window below him. He held his fire and waited.

At last, what he had been waiting for—hoping for—happened. First Darby and then Hoover, when they received no return fire for almost five minutes, darted out from behind the trees and raced across the street, obviously intending to storm the building.

Gabe took careful aim and squeezed the trigger. His round blasted into Darby's gut. The man was thrown backward. His hands flew up into the air, and his gun fell from his hand.

"Nooooo!" Hoover screamed without breaking stride as he glanced over his shoulder and saw Darby go down, another bloody body in the street. And then Hoover was out of sight, under the overhang in front of the building.

Gabe leaned over the parapet and peppered the overhang with shots that tore through it. Had he hit Hoover? There was no way of knowing, since he couldn't see the man from where he was. But Hoover was silent. If he had been hit, he might have made a sound. Unless one or more of Gabe's shots had killed him instantly.

A silence as loud as any thunder settled on the street and surrounding area. No shots sounded. No one was on the street. No people, no wagons, nothing. The silence gnawed at Gabe. It made him decidedly uneasy. So did the unsettling fact that there were three men—if Hoover was still alive—still after him and he didn't know where any of them were.

Then a shout came from behind him.

"Drop your goddamned gun, Conrad!"

He turned to face Abel Bates, who was standing opposite him on the far side of the roof, his gun held firmly in his hand, a scowl on his face.

"Drop it!" Abel yelled. He wasn't much older than his brother. "*Drop it, I said!*"

Gabe dropped his gun.

Abel began to smile. He slowly approached Gabe, his gun never once wavering.

"I figured you weren't where you started out at," he said as he continued advancing. "When I went inside the second floor and you weren't there, I figured there was only one place you could be. Up here."

Abel halted. He fired.

Gabe spun around and fell. He hit the roof hard. He grabbed the gun he had just been forced to drop and fired at Abel just as Abel fired a second time. This time Abel didn't miss. Abel's shot grazed Gabe's side, leaving a burning sensation behind it.

But Gabe's shot had hit its mark. Abel, a startled expression on his face, crumpled into a twisted heap on the roof.

Gabe's tactic had worked. Pretending to be hit by Abel's first round, he had gone down and achieved his purpose in going down—he had retrieved his gun and used it to eliminate Abel.

He rose and made his way past Abel's body to the edge of the roof. He climbed down and swung his legs through the window below him. As he entered the second floor, he blinked several times until his eyes became accustomed to the dim light.

That dim light was made suddenly brighter as fire blazed from the muzzle of a revolver held by a burly man perched on top of a tall stack of crates. His round almost got Gabe, who leapt to one side and returned fire. Then he quickly thumbed cartridges out of his belt and reloaded his revolver.

He leapt to his feet and, firing fast, rushed toward the stack of crates which supported the man who had to be Cousin Kane, since only he and Caleb Hoover had not been accounted for. Gabe threw himself against it, and as he had hoped, it teetered a moment and then toppled, throwing Kane to the floor. Gabe scrambled over the haphazard pile of crates, slipping and stumbling, until he was over the tumbled obstacles and had seized Kane by the throat with his free hand and was beginning to throttle him.

A shot came from behind him but whined harmlessly past his left ear. He spun around, swinging Kane with him so that Caleb Hoover's next shot, fired from the doorway leading to the second floor, hit Kane instead of Gabe.

The man went limp in Gabe's hand. His head dropped forward as his gun fell from his hand.

Gabe, still holding onto him and keeping his corpse positioned defensively in front of him, fired at Hoover.

Hoover fired back and again hit his relative.

As Cousin Kane's body lurched with the impact of the round it had just taken, Gabe shoved the corpse forward into the volley of shots Hoover was wildly firing, a demented gleam in his eye and a demonic expression on his face.

Cousin Kane's body went down. Gabe fired and hit Hoover in the chest. Hoover went down on his knees. He tried to squeeze the trigger of his gun as he stared dazed up at Gabe, who was standing his ground and watching him closely, ready to blast the man into eternity if and when that proved to be necessary.

It wasn't necessary.

Hoover fell forward. His face hit the floor.

Gabe stood there, staring at the bodies, thinking that his enemies' strategy hadn't been a bad one, although it hadn't worked. He was sure he knew what had happened. Abel Bates and Cousin Kane decided to run him down inside the building. They must have come to the second floor, seen he wasn't there, and then Abel went up to the roof to see if he had gone there while Cousin Kane had remained on the second floor in case he showed up there again. Later, Caleb Hoover and Ed Darby had decided to join forces with Abel and Kane.

He stepped over Hoover's body, holstering his gun as he did so, and went outside. He climbed down the steps and made his way back to the street, where he stood staring at the bodies, including his dapple's, which littered it.

He would buy himself another horse. He would move on. He didn't know where he was going, but he wanted to be away from the places he had recently been. Death haunted them.

But it no longer haunted him. He had disposed of the Hoover clan, who had been determined to kill him. He had nothing to fear anymore from Cathy Miller, who had also wanted to spill blood for blood.

And he had nothing more to fear now from anonymous bounty hunters since he was no longer wanted dead or alive by the law.

It was good to be free of the past's ghosts, he thought, as he headed down the corpse-strewn street.